und Andere, T. Moran

Songs of Nature

Selected from Many Sources

und Andere, T. Moran

Songs of Nature
Selected from Many Sources

ISBN/EAN: 9783744771368

Printed in Europe, USA, Canada, Australia, Japan

Cover: Foto ©Andreas Hilbeck / pixelio.de

More available books at **www.hansebooks.com**

Songs of Nature

SELECTED FROM MANY SOURCES,

WITH MANY ILLUSTRATIONS FROM ORIGINAL DESIGNS

BY

T. MORAN, MISS HALLOCK, CHURCH, FENN, PARSONS,
KENSETT, JOHNSON, BOLLES, Etc.

NEW YORK:

SCRIBNER, ARMSTRONG, AND COMPANY,

SUCCESSORS TO

CHARLES SCRIBNER AND COMPANY.

1873.

RIVERSIDE, CAMBRIDGE:
STEREOTYPED AND PRINTED BY
H. O. HOUGHTON AND COMPANY.

PUBLISHERS' NOTE.

The present volume completes the reissue of FOLK-SONGS, under the various titles of SONGS OF LIFE; SONGS OF HOME; SONGS OF THE HEART, and SONGS OF NATURE. The comprehensiveness and completeness of each part, with the numerous new forms and additional illustrations, has commended these selections anew to the public favor, and the four volumes now form a choice library of poetry and song.

CONTENTS.

vii

CONTENTS.

LIST OF ILLUSTRATIONS.

LIST OF ILLUSTRATIONS.

AUTOGRAPHS.

A FOREST HYMN.

THE groves were God's first temples. Ere man learned

To hew the shaft, and lay the architrave,
And spread the roof above them — ere he framed
The lofty vault, to gather and roll back
The sound of anthems; in the darkling wood,
Amid the cool and silence, he knelt down,
And offered to the Mightiest solemn thanks
And supplication. For his simple heart
Might not resist the sacred influences
Which, from the stilly twilight of the place,
And from the gray old trunks that high in heaven
Mingled their mossy boughs, and from the sound
Of the invisible breath that swayed at once
All their green tops, stole over him, and bowed
His spirit with the thought of boundless power
And inaccessible majesty. Ah, why
Should we, in the world's riper years, neglect
God's ancient sanctuaries, and adore
Only among the crowd, and under roofs
That our frail hands have raised? Let me, at least,
Here, in the shadow of this aged wood,
Offer one hymn — thrice happy, if it find
Acceptance in His ear.

                    Father, thy hand
Hath reared these venerable columns, thou
Didst weave this verdant roof. Thou didst look down
Upon the naked earth, and, forthwith, rose
All these fair ranks of trees. They, in thy sun,
Budded, and shook their green leaves in thy breeze,
And shot toward heaven. The century-living crow
Whose birth was in their tops, grew old and died

Among their branches, till, at last, they stood,
As now they stand, massy, and tall, and dark,
Fit shrine for humble worshipper to hold
Communion with his Maker. These dim vaults,
These winding aisles, of human pomp or pride
Report not. No fantastic carvings show
The boast of our vain race to change the form
Of thy fair works. But thou art here — thou fill'st
The solitude. Thou art in the soft winds
That run along the summit of these trees
In music ; thou art in the cooler breath
That from the inmost darkness of the place
Comes, scarcely felt ; the barky trunks, the ground,
The fresh moist ground, are all instinct with thee.
Here is continual worship ; — Nature, here,
In the tranquillity that thou dost love,
Enjoys thy presence. Noiselessly, around,
From perch to perch, the solitary bird
Passes ; and yon clear spring, that, midst its herbs,
Wells softly forth and wandering steeps the roots
Of half the mighty forest, tells no tale
Of all the good it does. Thou hast not left
Thyself without a witness, in these shades,
Of thy perfections. Grandeur, strength, and grace
Are here to speak of thee. This mighty oak —
By whose immovable stem I stand and seem
Almost annihilated — not a prince,
In all that proud old world beyond the deep,
E'er wore his crown as loftily as he
Wears the green coronal of leaves with which
Thy hand has graced him. Nestled at his root

Is beauty, such as blooms not in the glare
Of the broad sun. That delicate forest flower,
With scented breath and look so like a smile,
Seems, as it issues from the shapeless mould,
An emanation of the indwelling Life,
A visible token of the upholding Love,
That are the soul of this great universe.

My heart is awed within me when I think
Of the great miracle that still goes on,
In silence, round me — the perpetual work
Of thy creation, finished, yet renewed
Forever. Written on thy works I read
The lesson of thy own eternity.
Lo! all grow old and die — but see again,
How on the faltering footsteps of decay
Youth presses — ever gay and beautiful youth
In all its beautiful forms. These lofty trees
Wave not less proudly that their ancestors .
Moulder beneath them. O, there is not lost
One of earth's charms: upon her bosom yet,
After the flight of untold centuries,
The freshness of her far beginning lies
And yet shall lie. Life mocks the idle hate
Of his arch-enemy Death — yea, seats himself
Upon the tyrant's throne — the sepulchre,
And of the triumphs of his ghastly foe
Makes his own nourishment. For he came forth
From thine own bosom, and shall have no end.

There have been holy men who hid themselves
Deep in the woody wilderness, and gave

Their lives to thought and prayer, till they outlived
The generation born with them, nor seemed
Less aged than the hoary trees and rocks
Around them ; — and there have been holy men
Who deemed it were not well to pass life thus.
But let me often to these solitudes
Retire, and in thy presence reassure
My feeble virtue. Here its enemies,
The passions, at thy plainer footsteps shrink
And tremble and are still. O God! when thou
Dost scare the world with tempests, set on fire
The heavens with falling thunderbolts, or fill,
With all the waters of the firmament,
The swift dark whirlwind that uproots the woods
And drowns the villages ; when, at thy call,
Uprises the great deep and throws himself
Upon the continent, and overwhelms
Its cities — who forgets not, at the sight
Of these tremendous tokens of thy power,
His pride, and lays his strifes and follies by ?
O, from these sterner aspects of thy face
Spare me and mine, nor let us need the wrath
Of the mad unchained elements to teach
Who rules them. Be it ours to meditate,
In these calm shades, thy milder majesty,
And to the beautiful order of thy works
Learn to conform the order of our lives.

WILLIAM CULLEN BRYANT.

MIGNONETTE.

" Your qualities surpass your charms." — LANGUAGE OF FLOWERS.

I PASSED before her garden gate:
    She stood among her roses,
And stooped a little from the state
    In which her pride reposes,
To make her flowers a graceful plea
For luring and delaying me.

" When summer blossoms fade so soon,"
   She said with winning sweetness,
" Who does not wear the badge of June
   Lacks something of completeness.
My garden welcomes you to-day,
Come in and gather, while you may."

I entered in: she led me through
   A maze of leafy arches,
Where velvet-purple pansies grew
   Beneath the sighing larches, —
A shadowy, still, and cool retreat
That gave excuse for lingering feet.

She paused; pulled down a trailing vine;
   And twisted round her finger
Its starry sprays of jessamine,
   As one who seeks to linger.
But I smiled lightly in her face,
And passed on to the open space.

Passed many a flower bed fitly set
   In trim and blooming order,
And plucked at last some mignonette
   That strayed along the border;
A simple thing that had no bloom,
And but a faint and far perfume.

She wondered why I would not choose
   That dreamy amaryllis, —

MIGNONETTE.

"And could I really, then, refuse
   Those heavenly white lilies!
And leave ungathered on the slope
This passion-breathing heliotrope?"

She did not know — what need to tell
   So fair and fine a creature? —
That there was one who loved me well
   Of widely different nature;
A little maid whose tender youth,
And innocence, and simple truth,

Had won my heart with qualities
   That far surpassed her beauty,
And held me with unconscious ease
   Enthralled of love and duty;
Whose modest graces all were met
And symboled in my mignonette.

I passed outside her garden-gate,
   And left her proudly smiling:
Her roses bloomed too late, too late
   She saw, for my beguiling.
I wore instead — and wear it yet —
The single spray of mignonette.

Its fragrance greets me unaware,
   A vision clear recalling
Of shy, sweet eyes, and drooping hair
   In girlish tresses falling,

And little hands so white and fine
That timidly creep into mine ;

As she — all ignorant of the arts
    That wiser maids are plying —
Has crept into my heart of hearts
    Past doubting or denying ;
Therein, while suns shall rise and set,
To bloom unchanged, my Mignonette !

                                    MARY BRADLEY.

THE DYING LOVER.

THE grass that is under me now
    Will soon be over me sweet !
When you walk this way again,
    I shall not hear your feet.

You may walk this way again
    And shed your tears like dew :
They will be no more to me, then,
    Than mine are now to you.

                        RICHARD HENRY STODDARD.

PHILOMELA.

Hark! ah, the Nightingale!
The tawny-throated!
Hark! from that moonlit cedar what a burst!
What triumph! hark—what pain!
O wanderer from a Grecian shore,
Still, after many years, in distant lands,
Still nourishing in thy bewildered brain
That wild, unquenched, deep-sunken, old-world pain!
　　　Say, will it never heal?
And can this fragrant lawn,
With its cool trees, and night,
And the sweet, tranquil Thames,
And moonshine, and the dew,
To thy racked heart and brain
　　　Afford no balm?

　　　Dost thou to-night behold,
Here, through the moonlight on this English grass,
The unfriendly palace in the Thracian wild?
　　　Dost thou again peruse,
With hot cheeks and seared eyes,
The too clear web, and thy dumb sister's shame?
　　　Dost thou once more essay
Thy flight; and feel come over thee,
Poor fugitive, the feathery change,
Once more; and once more make resound,

10

With love and hate, triumph and agony,
Lone Daulis, and the high Cephisian vale?

Listen, Eugenia!
How thick the bursts come crowding through the leaves!
Again — thou hearest?
Eternal passion!
Eternal pain!

MATTHEW ARNOLD.

————•————

LUCY ASHTON'S SONG.

Look not thou on Beauty's charming;
Sit thou still when kings are arming;
Taste not when the wine-cup glistens;
Speak not when the people listens;
Stop thine ear against the singer;
From the red gold keep thy finger:
Vacant heart and hand and eye
Easy live, and quiet die.

SIR WALTER SCOTT.

SPRING AND WINTER.

I.

WHEN daisies pied, and violets blue,
    And lady-smocks all silver-white,
And cuckoo-buds of yellow hue,
    Do paint the meadows with delight,
The cuckoo then, on every tree,
Mocks married men, for thus sings he:
        Cuckoo!
Cuckoo, cuckoo!—O word of fear,
Unpleasing to a married ear!

When shepherds pipe on oaten straws,
    And merry larks are ploughmen's clocks,
When turtles tread, and rooks, and daws,
    And maidens bleach their summer smocks.
The cuckoo then, on every tree,
Mocks married men, for thus sings he:
        Cuckoo!
Cuckoo, cuckoo!—O word of fear,
Unpleasing to a married ear!

II.

When icicles hang by the wall,
    And Dick the shepherd blows his nail,
And Tom bears logs into the hall,
    And milk comes frozen home in pail,

12

When blood is nipped, and ways be foul,
Then nightly sings the staring owl ·
          To-who!
Tu-whit, to-who! — a merry note,
While greasy Jean doth keel the pot.

When all aloud the wind doth blow,
    And coughing drowns the parson's saw,
And birds sit brooding in the snow,
    And Marian's nose looks red and raw ;
When roasted crabs hiss in the bowl,
Then nightly sings the staring owl :
          To-who!
Tu-whit, to-who! — a merry note,
While greasy Joan doth keel the pot.
                                    SHAKESPEARE.

SABINA.

SEE, see! She wakes — Sabina wakes!
    And now the sun begins to rise:
Less glorious is the morn that breaks
    From his bright beams than her fair eyes.

With light united, Day they give ;
    But different fates ere night fulfill :
How many by his warmth will live!
    How many will her coldness kill !
                        WILLIAM CONGREVE.

WIND AND RAIN.

RATTLE the window, Winds!
  Rain, drip on the panes!
There are tears and sighs in our hearts and eyes,
  And a weary weight on our brains.

The gray sea heaves and heaves,
  On the dreary flats of sand;
And the blasted limb of the churchyard yew,
  It shakes like a ghostly hand!

The dead are engulfed beneath it,
  Sunk in the grassy waves;
But we have more dead in our hearts to-day
  Than the Earth in all her graves!

RICHARD HENRY STODDARD.

THE BELFRY PIGEON.

On the cross-beam under the Old South bell
The nest of a pigeon is builded well.
In summer and winter that bird is there,
Out and in with the morning air.
I love to see him track the street,
With his wary eye and active feet;
And I often watch him as he springs,
Circling the steeple with easy wings,
Till across the dial his shade has passed,
And the belfry edge is gained at last.
'Tis a bird I love, with its brooding note,
And the trembling throb in its mottled throat;
There's a human look in its swelling breast,
And the gentle curve of its lowly crest;
And I often stop with the fear I feel,
He runs so close to the rapid wheel.

Whatever is rung on that noisy bell,
Chime of the hour, or funeral knell,
The dove in the belfry must hear it well.
When the tongue swings out to the midnight moon,
When the sexton cheerly rings for noon,
When the clock strikes clear at morning light,
When the child is waked with "nine at night,"
When the chimes play soft in the Sabbath air,
Filling the spirit with tones of prayer,

15

Whatever tale in the bell is heard,
He broods on his folded feet unstirred,
Or, rising half in his rounded nest,
He takes the time to smooth his breast ;
Then drops again, with filmed eyes,
And sleeps as the last vibration dies.

   Sweet bird ! I would that I could be
A hermit in the crowd like thee !
With wings to fly to wood and glen,
Thy lot, like mine, is cast with men ;
And daily, with unwilling feet,
I tread, like thee, the crowded street ;
But, unlike me, when day is o'er,
Thou canst dismiss the world, and soar ;
Or, at a half-felt wish for rest,
Canst smooth the feathers on thy breast,
And drop, forgetful, to thy nest.

   I would that, in such wings of gold,
I could my weary heart upfold ;
I would I could look down unmoved,
(Unloving as I am unloved,)
And while the world throngs on beneath,
Smooth down my cares and calmly breathe ;
And never sad with others' sadness,
And never glad with others' gladness,
Listen, unstirred, to knell or chime,
And, lapped in quiet, bide my time.

NATHANIEL PARKER WILLIS.

THE SHEPHERD'S SON.

THE gowan glitters on the sward,
    The lavrock's in the sky,
And Colley on my plaid keeps ward,
    And time is passing by.
    O no! sad and slow!
    I hear nae welcome sound;
The shadow of our trysting bush,
    It wears sae slowly round.

My sheep-bell tinkles from the west,
    My lambs are bleating near;
But still the sound that I lo'e best
    Alack! I canna hear.
    O no! sad and slow!
    The shadow lingers still,
And like a lanely ghaist I stand,
    And croon upon the hill.

I hear below the water roar,
    The mill with clacking din;
And Lucky scolding frae her door,
    To bring the bairnies in.
    O no! sad and slow!
    These are nae sounds for me;
The shadow of our trysting bush,
    It creeps sae drearilie.

I coft yestreen frae chapman Tam
    A snood o' bonnie blue,
And promised, when our trysting cam.
    To tie it round her brow.
    O no! sad and slow!
    The time it winna pass;
The shadow of that weary thorn
    Is tethered on the grass.

O now I see her on the way!
    She's past the witches' knowe;
She's climbing up the brownie's brae:
    My heart is in a lowe!
    O no! 'tis not so!
    'Tis glaumrie I hae seen;
The shadow of the hawthorn bush
    Will move nae mair till e'en.

My book of grace I'll try to read,
    Though conned wi' little skill;
When Colley barks I'll raise my head,
    And find her on the hill.
    O no! sad and slow!
    The time will ne'er be gane;
The shadow of the trysting bush
    Is fixed like ony stane.

JOANNA BAILLIE.

'ER the gray old German city
   The shadow of mourning lay:
More tenderly kissed each mother
   Her little child that day.

With a deeper prayer each father
   Laid his hand on his first-born's head,
For in the castle above them
   Lay the Count's little daughter, dead.

Slow moved the great procession
   Down from the castle gate,
To where the black-draped cathedral
   Blazed in funereal state.

19

And they laid the little child down,
  In her robes of satin and gold,
To sleep with her dead forefathers
  In their stone crypt, dark and cold.

At midnight the Countess lay weeping
  'Neath her gorgeous canopy,
She heard as it were a rustling,
  And little feet come nigh.

She started up in the darkness,
  And with yearning gesture wild,
She cried, " Has the Father heard me?
  Art thou come back, my child? "

Then a child's voice, soft and pleading,
  Said, " I've come, O mother dear,

To ask if you will not lay me
Where the little birds I can hear; —

" The little birds in their singing,
And the children in their play,
Where the sun shines bright on the flowers
All the long summer day.

" In the stone crypt I lie weeping,
For I cannot choose but fear,
Such wailings dire and ceaseless
From the dead Counts' coffins I hear.

" And I'm all alone, dear mother,
No other child is there;
O, lay me to sleep in the sunshine,
Where all is bright and fair.

" I cannot stay, dear mother,
    I must back to the moans and gloom ;
I must lie there, fearing and weeping,
    Till you take me from my tomb."

Then the Countess roused her husband,
    Saying, " Give to me, I pray,
That spot of green by the deep fosse,
    Where the children love to play.

" For our little one lies weeping,
    And asks, for Christ's dear sake,
That 'mid song and sunlight and flowers,
    Near children her grave we make."

And the green spot was made a garden,
    Blessed by priests with book and prayer,

And they laid the Count's little daughter
  ' Mid flowers and sunlight there.

And to the children forever
  The Count and Countess gave
As a play-ground, that smiling garden
  By their little daughter's grave.

MRS. R. S. GREENOUGH.

THE HOLLY TREE.

O READER! hast thou ever stood to see
    The holly tree?
The eye that contemplates it well, perceives
    Its glossy leaves
Ordered by an intelligence so wise
As might confound the atheist's sophistries.

Below, a circling fence, its leaves are seen
  Wrinkled and keen;
No grazing cattle, through their prickly round,
  Can reach to wound;
But as they grow where nothing is to fear,
Smooth and unarmed the pointless leaves appear.

I love to view these things with curious eyes,
  And moralize;
And in this wisdom of the holly tree
  Can emblems see
Wherewith, perchance, to make a pleasant rhyme,
One which may profit in the after-time.

Thus, though abroad, perchance, I might appear
  Harsh and austere,
To those who on my leisure would intrude
  Reserved and rude;
Gentle at home, amid my friends, I'd be,
Like the high leaves upon the holly tree.

And should my youth, as youth is apt I know,
  Some harshness show,
All vain asperities I, day by day,
  Would wear away,
Till the smooth temper of my age should be
Like the high leaves upon the holly tree.

And as, when all the summer trees are seen
  So bright and green,

The holly leaves their fadeless hues display
    Less bright than they;
But when the bare and wintry woods we see,
What then so cheerful as the holly tree?

So, serious should my youth appear among
    The thoughtless throng;
So would I seem, amid the young and gay,
    More grave than they;
That in my age as cheerful I might be
As the green winter of the holly tree.

ROBERT SOUTHEY.

———◆———

THE NYMPH COMPLAINING FOR THE DEATH OF HER FAWN

THE wanton troopers, riding by,
Have shot my fawn, and it will die.
Ungentle men! they cannot thrive,
Who killed thee. Thou ne'er didst, alive,
Them any harm; alas! nor could
Thy death yet do them any good.
I'm sure I never wished them ill,
Nor do I for all this, nor will;
But, if my simple prayers may yet
Prevail with Heaven to forget
Thy murder, I will join my tears,
Rather than fail. But O, my fears!

It cannot die so.   Heaven's King
Keeps register of everything,
And nothing may we use in vain;
Even beasts must be with justice slain,
Else men are made their deodands.
Though they should wash their guilty hands
In this warm life-blood, which doth part
From thine and wound me to the heart,
Yet could they not be clean — their stain
Is dyed in such a purple grain;
There is not such another in
The world, to offer for their sin.

   Inconstant Sylvio! when yet
I had not found him counterfeit,
One morning (I remember well),
Tied in this silver chain and bell,
Gave it to me.   Nay, and I know
What he said then — I'm sure I do:
Said he, "Look how your huntsman here
Hath taught a fawn to hunt his dear!"
But Sylvio soon had me beguiled:
This waxed tame, while he grew wild;
And, quite regardless of my smart,
Left me his fawn, but took his heart.
   Thenceforth, I set myself to play
My solitary time away,
With this; and, very well content,
Could so mine idle life have spent.
For it was full of sport, and light
Of foot and heart, and did invite
Me to its game.   It seemed to bless

Itself in me; how could I less
Than love it? O! I cannot be
Unkind t' a beast that loveth me.

Had it lived long, I do not know
Whether it, too, might have done so
As Sylvio did — his gifts might be
Perhaps as false, or more, than he.
For I am sure, for aught that I
Could in so short a time espy,
Thy love was far more better than
The love of false and cruel man.

With sweetest milk, and sugar, first
I it at mine own fingers nursed;
And as it grew, so every day
It waxed more white and sweet than they.
It had so sweet a breath! and oft
I blushed to see its foot more soft
And white — shall I say than my hand?
Nay! any lady's of the land.

It is a wondrous thing how fleet
'Twas, on those little silver feet!
With what a pretty, skipping grace
It oft would challenge me the race!
And when 't had left me far away,
'Twould stay, and run again, and stay;
For it was nimbler, much, than hinds,
And trod as if on the four winds.

I have a garden of my own,
But so with roses overgrown,
And lilies, that you would it guess
To be a little wilderness;

And all the spring-time of the year
It only loved to be there.
Among the beds of lilies I
Have sought it oft, where it should lie ;
Yet could not, till itself would rise,
Find it, although before mine eyes ;
For in the flaxen lilies' shade
It like a bank of lilies laid.
Upon the roses it would feed,
Until its lips ev'n seemed to bleed ;
And then to me 'twould boldly trip,
And print those roses on my lip.
But all its chief delight was still
On roses thus itself to fill,
And its pure virgin limbs to fold
In whitest sheets of lilies cold.
Had it lived long, it would have been
Lilies without, roses within.

O help ! O help ! I see it faint,
And die as calmly as a saint !
See, how it weeps ! the tears do come,
Sad, slowly, dropping like a gum.
So weeps the wounded balsam ; so
The holy frankincense doth flow ;
The brotherless Heliades
Melt in such amber tears as these.

I in a golden vial will
Keep these two crystal tears, and fill
It, till it do o'erflow, with mine ;
Then place it in Diana's shrine.

Now my sweet fawn is vanished to

Whither the swans and turtles go,
In fair Elysium to endure,
With milk-white lambs, and ermins pure.
O do not run too fast! for I
Will but bespeak thy grave — and die.
  First, my unhappy statue shall
Be cut in marble; and withal,
Let it be weeping too.   But there
Th' engraver sure his art may spare;
For I so truly thee bemoan,
That I shall weep, though I be stone,
Until my tears, still drooping, wear
My breast, themselves engraving there.
There at my feet shalt thou be laid,
Of purest alabaster made;
For I would have thine image be
White as I can, though not as thee.

ANDREW MARVELL.

COME, BEAUTEOUS DAY.

  COME, beauteous day!
Never did lover on his bridal night
So chide thine over-eager light
  As I thy long delay!

Bring me my rest!
Never can these sweet thorny roses,
Whereon my heart reposes,
　Be into slumber pressed.

　Day be my night!
Night hath no stars to rival with her eyes;
Night hath no peace like his who lies
　Upon her bosom white.

　She did transmute
This my poor cell into a paradise,
Gorgeous with blossoming lips and dewy eyes,
　And all her beauty's fruit.

　Nor dull nor gray
Seems to mine eyes this dim and wintry morn:
Ne'er did the rosy banners of the dawn
　Herald a brighter day.

　Come, beauteous day!
Come! or in sunny light, or storm eclipse!
Bring me the immortal Summer of her lips;
　Then have thy way!

WILLIAM HENRY HURLBUT.

THE NIGHT PIECE.

HER eyes the glow-worme lend thee.
The shooting-starres attend thee;
    And the elves also,
    Whose little eyes glow
Like the sparks of fire, befriend thee.

No Will-o'-th'-Wispe mislight thee,
Nor snake nor slow-worme bite thee;
    But on thy way,
    Not making stay,
Since ghost there's none t' affright thee.

Let not the darke thee cumber;
What though the moon does slumber?
    The stars of the night
    Will lend thee their light,
Like tapers cleare, without number.

Then, Julia, let me woo thee,
Thus, thus to come unto me;
    And when I shall meet
    Thy silvery feet,
My soule I'll pour into thee!

ROBERT HERRICK.

31

Thanks awin birthnight! be the festive East,
The uneasy wind moans with its sense of cold,
And sends its sighs through gloomy mountain-gorge,
Along the valley, up the whitening hill,
To rouse the sighing spirits of the pines,
And wail in distance round their chilly life.

E. O. Wallcutt

A WINTER SCENE.

WINTER'S wild birthnight! In the fretful East
The uneasy wind moans with its sense of cold,
And sends its sighs through gloomy mountain gorge,
Along the valley, up the whitening hill,
To tease the sighing spirits of the pines,
And waste in dismal woods their chilly life.
The sky is dark, and on the huddled leaves —
The restless, rustling leaves — sifts down its sleet,
Till the sharp crystals pin them to the earth,
And they grow still beneath the rising storm.
The roofless bullock hugs the sheltering stack,
With cringing head and closely gathered feet,
And waits with dumb endurance for the morn.
Deep in a gusty cavern of the barn
The witless calf stands blatant at his chain;
While the brute mother, pent within her stall,
With the wild stress of instinct goes distraught,
And frets her horns, and bellows through the night.
The stream runs black; and the far waterfall,
That sang so sweetly through the summer eves,
And swelled and swayed to Zephyr's softest breath,
Leaps with a sullen roar the dark abyss,
And howls its hoarse responses to the wind.
The mill is still. The distant factory,
That swarmed yestreen with many fingered life,
And bridged the river with a hundred bars

C   33

Of molten light, is dark, and lifts its bulk
With dim, uncertain angles, to the sky.

.   .   .   .

Yet lower bows the storm. The leafless trees
Lash their lithe limbs, and with majestic voice,
Call to each other through the deepening gloom;
And slender trunks that lean on burly boughs
Shriek with the sharp abrasion; and the oak,
Mellowed in fibre by unnumbered frosts,
Yields to the shoulder of the Titan Blast,
Forsakes its poise, and, with a booming crash,
Sweeps a fierce passage to the smothered rocks,
And lies a shattered ruin.

JOSIAH GILBERT HOLLAND.

UP IN THE TREE.

WHAT would you see, if I took you up
　　My little aerie-stair?
You would see the sky like a clear blue cup
　　Turned upside down in the air.

What would you do, up my aerie-stair,
　　In my little nest on the tree?
My child with cries would trouble the air,
　　To get what she could but see.

What would you get in the top of the tree,
   For all your crying and grief?
Not a star would you clutch of all you see —
   You could only gather a leaf.

But when you had lost your greedy grief,
   Content to see from afar,
You would find in your hand a withering leaf,
   In your heart a shining star.

GEORGE MACDONALD.

———•———

HYMN TO THE FLOWERS.

DAY-STARS! that ope your eyes with morn to twinkle
   From rainbow galaxies of earth's creation,
And dew-drops on her lonely altars sprinkle
     As a libation!

Ye matin worshippers! who bending lowly
   Before the uprisen sun — God's lidless eye —
Throw from your chalices a sweet and holy
     Incense on high!

Ye bright mosaics! that with storied beauty
The floor of Nature's temple tessellate:
What numerous emblems of instructive duty
Your forms create!

'Neath cloistered boughs, each floral bell that swingeth,
And tolls its perfume on the passing air,
Makes Sabbath in the fields, and ever ringeth
A call to prayer.

Not to the domes where crumbling arch and column
  Attest the feebleness of mortal hand,
But to that fane, most catholic and solemn,
        Which God hath planned:

To that cathedral, boundless as our wonder,
  Whose quenchless lamps the sun and moon supply —
Its choir the winds and waves, its organ thunder,
        Its dome the sky.

There — as in solitude and shade I wander
  Through the green aisles, or, stretched upon the sod,
Awed by the silence, reverently ponder
        The ways of God —

Your voiceless lips, O Flowers, are living preachers,
  Each cup a pulpit, and each leaf a book,
Supplying to my fancy numerous teachers
        From loneliest nook.

Floral Apostles! that in dewy splendor
  "Weep without woe, and blush without a crime,"
O may I deeply learn, and ne'er surrender,
        Your lore sublime!

"Thou wert not, Solomon, in all thy glory,
  Arrayed," the lilies cry, "in robes like ours:
How vain your grandeur! Ah, how transitory
        Are human flowers!"

In the sweet-scented pictures, Heavenly Artist,
   With which thou paintest Nature's wide-spread hall,
What a delightful lesson thou impartest
       Of love to all!

Not useless are ye, Flowers! though made for pleasure ·
   Blooming o'er field and wave, by day and night,
From every source your sanction bids me treasure
       Harmless delight.

Ephemeral sages! what instructors hoary
   For such a world of thought could furnish scope?
Each fading calyx a *memento mori*,
       Yet fount of hope.

Posthumous glories! angel-like collection!
   Upraised from seed or bulb interred in earth,
Ye are to me a type of resurrection,
       And second birth.

Were I, O God, in churchless lands remaining,
   Far from all voice of teachers or divines,
My soul would find, in flowers of Thy ordaining,
       Priests, sermons, shrines!

                       HORACE SMITH.

SONG TO MAY.

MAY! queen of blossoms,
    And fulfilling flowers,
With what pretty music
    Shall we charm the hours?
Wilt thou have pipe and reed,
Blown in the open mead?
Or to the lute give heed,
    In the green bowers?

Thou hast no need of us,
    Or pipe or wire,
That hast the golden bee
    Ripened with fire;
And many thousand more
Songsters, that thee adore,
Filling earth's grassy floor
    With new desire.

Thou hast thy mighty herds,
    Tame, and free livers;
Doubt not, thy music too
    In the deep rivers;
And the whole plumy flight.
Warbling the day and night:
Up at the gates of light,
    See, the lark quivers!

When with the jacinth
    Coy fountains are tressed,
And for the mournful bird
    Greenwoods are dressed,
That did for Tereus pine,
Then shall our songs be thine,
To whom our hearts incline :
    May, be thou blessed !

LORD THURLOW

————◆————

THE RHODORA.

In May, when sea-winds pierced our solitudes,
I found the fresh Rhodora in the woods,
Spreading its leafless blooms in a damp nook,
To please the desert and the sluggish brook :
The purple petals, fallen in the pool,
    Made the black waters with their beauty gay ;
Here might the red-bird come his plumes to cool,
    And court the flower that cheapens his array.
Rhodora ! if the sages ask thee why
This charm is wasted on the marsh and sky,
Dear, tell them that if eyes were made for seeing,
Then beauty is its own excuse for being.
    Why thou wert there, O rival of the rose !
I never thought to ask, I never knew ;
    But in my simple ignorance suppose
The selfsame Power that brought me there, brought you.

RALPH WALDO EMERSON.

THE FAIRIES.

Up the airy mountain,
  Down the rushy glen,
We daren't go a hunting,
  For fear of little men;
Wee folk, good folk,
  Trooping all together;
Green jacket, red cap,
  And white owl's feather!

Down along the rocky shore
  Some make their home:
They live on crispy pancakes
  Of yellow tide-foam;
Some in the reeds
  Of the black mountain-lake,
With frogs for their watch-dogs,
  All night awake.

High on the hill-top
  The old king sits;
He is now so old and gray
  He's nigh lost his wits.
With a bridge of white mist
  Columbkill he crosses,

On his stately journeys
  From Slieveleague to Rosses;
Or going up with music,
  On cold, starry nights,
To sup with the queen
  Of the gay Northern Lights.

They stole little Bridget
  For seven years long;
When she came down again
  Her friends were all gone.
They took her lightly back,
  Between the night and morrow;
They thought that she was fast asleep
  But she was dead with sorrow.
They have kept her ever since
  Deep within the lakes,
On a bed of flag-leaves,
  Watching till she wakes.

By the craggy hill-side,
  Through the mosses bare,
They have planted thorn-trees
  For pleasure here and there;
Is any man so daring
  To dig one up in spite,
He shall find the thornies set
  In his bed at night.

Up the airy mountain,
  Down the rushy glen,

We daren't go a hunt-
ing,
For fear of little
men ;
Wee folk, good folk,
Trooping all together ;
Green jacket, red cap,
And white owl's
feather !

WILLIAM ALLINGHAM.

SUMMER DAYS.

In Summer, when the days were long,
We walked together in the wood:
Our heart was light, our step was strong;
Sweet flutterings were there in our blood,
In Summer, when the days were long.

We strayed from morn till evening came;
We gathered flowers, and wove us crowns;
We walked 'mid poppies red as flame,
Or sat upon the yellow downs,
And always wished our life the same.

In Summer, when the days were long,
We leaped the hedgerow, crossed the brook;
And still her voice flowed forth in song,
Or else she read some graceful book,
In Summer, when the days were long.

And then we sat beneath the trees,
With shadows lessening in the noon;
And, in the sunlight and the breeze,
We feasted, many a gorgeous June,
While larks were singing o'er the leas.

44

In Summer, when the days were long,
On dainty chicken, snow-white bread,
We feasted, with no grace but song.
We plucked wild strawberries, ripe and red,
In Summer, when the days were long.

We loved, and yet we knew it not;
For loving seemed like breathing then.
We found a heaven in every spot,
Saw angels too, in all good men,
And dreamed of God in grove and grot.

In Summer, when the days are long,
Alone I wander, muse alone.
I see her not; but that old song
Under the fragrant wind is blown,
In Summer, when the days are long.

Alone I wander in the wood;
But one fair spirit hears my sighs;
And half I see, so glad and good,
The honest daylight of her eyes,
That charmed me under earlier skies.

In Summer, when the days are long,
I love her as we loved of old;
My heart is light, my step is strong;
For love brings back those hours of gold,
In Summer, when the days are long.

ANONYMOUS.

THE VIOLET.

O FAINT, delicious, spring-time violet,
        Thine odor, like a key,
Turns noiselessly in memory's wards, to let
        A thought of sorrow free!

The breath of distant fields upon my brow
        Blows through that open door
The sound of wind-borne bells, more sweet and low
        And sadder than of yore.

It comes afar, from that beloved place,
        And that beloved hour,
When life hung ripening in love's golden grace,
        Like grapes above a bower.

A spring goes singing through its reedy grass;
        The lark sings o'er my head,
Drowned in the sky — O pass, ye visions, pass!
        I would that I were dead!

Why hast thou opened that forbidden door
        From which I ever flee?
O vanished Joy! O Love, that art no more,
        Let my vexed spirit be!

O violet! thine odor through my brain
        Hath searched, and stung to grief
This sunny day, as if a curse did stain
        Thy velvet leaf.
                        WILLIAM WETMORE STORY.

ROSALIND'S MADRIGAL.

LOVE in my bosom, like a bee,
　　Doth suck his sweet;
Now with his wings he plays with me.
　　Now with his feet;
Within mine eyes he makes his nest,
His bed amidst my tender breast;
My kisses are his daily feast;
And yet he robs me of my rest:
　　Ah, wanton! will ye?

And if I sleep, then percheth he
　　With pretty flight,
And makes his pillow of my knee
　　The livelong night.
Strike I my lute, he tunes the string;
He music plays if so I sing;
He lends me every lovely thing;
Yet cruel he my heart doth sting:
　　Whist, wanton! still ye!

Else I with roses every day
　　Will whip you hence,
And bind you when you long to play.
　　For your offence;

I'll shut mine eyes to keep you in,
I'll make you fast it for your sin,
I'll count your power not worth a pin :
Alas ! what hereby shall I win
    If he gainsay me ?

What if I beat the wanton boy,
    With many a rod ?
He will repay me with annoy,
    Because a god.
Then sit thou safely on my knee,
And let thy bower my bosom be ;
Lurk in mine eyes — I like of thee.
O Cupid, so thou pity me,
    Spare not, but play thee !

              THOMAS LODGE.

VIRTUE.

SWEET day ! so cool, so calm, so bright,
The bridal of the earth and sky !
The dew shall weep thy fall to-night ;
    For thou must die.

Sweet rose ! whose hue, angry and brave,
Bids the rash gazer wipe his eye,
Thy root is ever in its grave ;
    And thou must die.

Sweet spring! full of sweet days and roses,
A box where sweets compacted lie,
Thy music shows ye have your closes;
    And all must die.

Only a sweet and virtuous soul,
Like seasoned timber, never gives;
But though the whole world turn to coal,
    Then chiefly lives.

GEORGE HERBERT.

SONG.

THE world goes up, and the world goes down,
  And the sunshine follows the rain;
And yesterday's sneer and yesterday's frown
  Can never come over again,
        Sweet wife,
  No, never come over again.

For woman is warm though man be cold,
  And the night will hallow the day;
Till the heart which at even was weary and old
  Can rise in the morning gay,
        Sweet wife,
  To its work in the morning gay.

CHARLES KINGSLEY.

D

THE BROOK-SIDE.

I WANDERED by the brook-side,
  I wandered by the mill;
I could not hear the brook flow,
  The noisy wheel was still;
There was no burr of grasshopper,
  No chirp of any bird;
But the beating of my own heart
  Was all the sound I heard.

I sat beneath the elm-tree ;
I watched the long, long shade,
And, as it grew still longer,
I did not feel afraid ;
For I listened for a footfall,
I listened for a word ;
But the beating of my own heart
Was all the sound I heard.

He came not — no, he came not ;
The night came on alone :
The little stars sat, one by one,
Each on his golden throne ;
The evening wind passed by my cheek,
The leaves above were stirred ;
But the beating of my own heart
Was all the sound I heard.

Fast silent tears were flowing,
When something stood behind ;
A hand was on my shoulder,
I knew its touch was kind :
It drew me nearer — nearer,
We did not speak one word ;
For the beating of our own hearts
Was all the sound we heard.

RICHARD MONCKTON MILNES.

LITTLE BELL.

He prayeth well, who loveth well
Both man and bird and beast.

"THE ANCIENT MARINER."

PIPED the blackbird on the beechwood spray:
" Pretty maid, slow wandering this way,
 What's your name?" quoth he;
" What's your name? O stop, and straight unfold,
Pretty maid with showery curls of gold."
 " Little Bell," said she.

Little Bell sat down beneath the rocks,
Tossed aside her gleaming golden locks:
 " Bonny bird," quoth she,
" Sing me your best song before I go."
" Here's the very finest song I know,
 Little Bell," said he.

And the blackbird piped; you never heard
Half so gay a song from any bird,
 Full of quips and wiles:
Now so round and rich, now soft and slow;
All for love of that sweet face below,
 Dimpled o'er with smiles.

And the while the bonny bird did pour
His full heart out freely, o'er and o'er,
  'Neath the morning skies,
In the little childish heart below
All the sweetness seemed to grow and grow,
And shine forth in happy overflow
  From the blue, bright eyes.

Down the dell she tripped, and through the glade;
Peeped the squirrel from the hazel shade,
  And from out the tree
Swung, and leaped, and frolicked, void of fear;
While bold blackbird piped that all might hear,
  " Little Bell!" piped he.

Little Bell sat down amid the fern;
" Squirrel, squirrel, to your task return:
  Bring me nuts!" quoth she.
Up, away the frisky squirrel hies,
Golden wood-lights glancing in his eyes,
  And adown the tree,
Great ripe nuts, kissed brown by July sun,
In the little lap dropped one by one;
Hark, how blackbird pipes to see the fun '
  " Happy Bell!" pipes he.

Little Bell looked up and down the glade:
" Squirrel, squirrel, if you're not afraid,
  Come and share with me!"
Down came squirrel, eager for his fare,
Down came bonny blackbird I declare.

Little Bell gave each his honest share:
   Ah, the merry three!

And the while these frolic playmates twain
Piped, and frisked from bough to bough again,
   'Neath the morning skies,
In the little childish heart below
All the sweetness seemed to grow and grow,
And shine out in happy overflow,
   From the blue, bright eyes.

By her snow-white cot at close of day,
Knelt sweet Bell, with folded palms, to pray.
   Very calm and clear
Rose the praying voice to where, unseen,
In blue heaven, an angel shape serene
   Paused awhile to hear.

" What good child is this," the angel said,
" That, with happy heart, beside her bed
   Prays so lovingly?"
Low and soft, O very low and soft!
Crooned the blackbird in the orchard croft:
   " Bell, dear Bell!" crooned he.

" Whom God's creatures love," the angel fair
Murmured, " God doth bless with angels' care;
   Child, thy bed shall be
Folded safe from harm. — Love deep and kind
Shall watch around, and leave good gifts behind,
   Little Bell, for thee.".   Thomas Westwood.

THE FADED VIOLET.

WHAT thought is folded in thy leaves !
  What tender thought, what speechless pain !
I hold thy faded lips to mine,
  Thou darling of the April rain.

I hold thy faded lips to mine,
  Though scent and azure tint are fled ;
O ! dry, mute lips, ye are the type
  Of something in me cold and dead :

Of something wilted like thy leaves,
  Of fragrance flown, of beauty dim ;
Yet, for the love of those white hands
  That found thee by a river's brim,

That found thee when thy sunny mouth
  Was purpled, as with drinking wine :
For love of her who love forgot,
  I hold thy faded lips to mine.

That thou shouldst live when I am dead,
  When hate is dead for me, and wrong,
For this I use my subtlest art,
  For this I fold thee in my song.

                    THOMAS BAILEY ALDRICH.

The Mountain Mistress.

By scattered rocks and turbid waters drifting
By furrowed glade and dell,
To foreign men thy calm, sweet face uplifting
Hon obliged them to tell

The delicate triumph, that cannot find expression
For none speak too fair,
That, like thy petals, trembles in possession
And scatters on the air.

THE MOUNTAIN HEART'S-EASE.

By scattered rocks and turbid waters shifting,
  By furrowed glade and dell,
To feverish men thy calm, sweet face uplifting,
  Thou stayest them to tell

The delicate thought, that cannot find expression,
  For ruder speech too fair,
That, like thy petals, trembles in possession,
  And scatters on the air.

The miner pauses in his rugged labor,
  And, leaning on his spade,
Laughingly calls unto his comrade neighbor
  To see thy charms displayed ;

But in his eyes a mist unwonted rises,
  And for a moment clear,
Some sweet home-face his foolish thought surprises
  And passes in a tear, —

Some boyish vision of his Eastern village,
  Of uneventful toil,
Where golden harvests followed quiet tillage
  Above a peaceful soil:

One moment only, for the pick, uplifting,
   Through root and fibre cleaves,
And on the muddy current slowly drifting
   Are swept thy bruisèd leaves.

And yet, O poet, in thy homely fashion
   Thy work thou dost fulfill,
For on the turbid current of his passion
   Thy face is shining still!

BRET HARTE.

—————◆—————

TIDES.

O PATIENT shore, that canst not go to meet
   Thy love, the restless sea, how comfortest
   Thou all thy loneliness? Art thou at rest,
When, loosing his strong arms from round thy feet,
He turns away? Know'st thou, however sweet
   That other shore may be, that to thy breast
   He must return? And when in sterner test
He folds thee to a heart which does not beat,
   Wraps thee in ice, and gives no smile, no kiss,
   To break long wintry days, still dost thou miss
Naught from thy trust? Still wait, unfaltering,
The higher, warmer waves which leap in spring?
O sweet, wise shore, to be so satisfied!
O heart, learn from the shore! Love has a tide!

II. II.

TO PRIMROSES.

FILLED WITH MORNING DEW.

WHY do ye weep, sweet babes? Can tears
    Speak grief in you,
      Who were but born
      Just as the modest morn
    Teemed her refreshing dew?
Alas! ye have not known that shower
    That mars a flower,
      Nor felt the unkind
      Breath of a blasting wind;
    Nor are ye worn with years,
    Or warped, as we,
    Who think it strange to see
Such pretty flowers, like to orphans young,
Speaking by tears before ye have a tongue.

Speak, whimpering younglings! and make known
    The reason why
      Ye droop and weep.
      Is it for want of sleep,
    Or childish lullaby?
Or that ye have not seen as yet
    The violet?
      Or brought a kiss
      From that sweetheart to this?

No, no; this sorrow, shown
By your tears shed,
Would have this lecture read:
" That things of greatest, so of meanest worth,
Conceived with grief are. and with tears brought forth.'

ROBERT HERRICK

———◆———

TO BLOSSOMS.

FAIR pledges of a fruitful tree,
    Why do ye fall so fast?
    Your date is not so past
But you may stay yet here awhile,
    To blush and gently smile,
        And go at last.

What! were ye born to be
    An hour or half's delight,
    And so to bid good-night?
'Tis pity Nature brought ye forth,
    Merely to show your worth,
        And lose you quite.

But you are lovely leaves, where we
    May read how soon things have
    Their end, though ne'er so brave ;
And, after they have shown their pride
    Like you awhile, they glide
        Into the grave.

ROBERT HERRICK

TO DAFFODILS

Fair daffodils, we weep to see
    You haste away so soon;
As yet the early-rising sun
    Has not attained his noon:
        Stay, stay
    Until the hastening day
        Has run
    But to the even-song;
And, having prayed together, we
    Will go with you along.

We have short time to stay as you;
    We have as short a Spring,
As quick a growth to meet decay,
    As you, or anything.
        We die,
    As your hours do; and dry
        Away
    Like to the Summer's rain,
Or as the pearls of morning dew:
    Ne'er to be found again.

                Robert Herrick.

THE MOTHER NIGHTINGALE

I HAVE seen a nightingale
On a sprig of thyme bewail,
Seeing the dear nest, which was
Hers alone, borne off, alas!
By a laborer; I heard,
For this outrage, the poor bird
Say a thousand mournful things
To the wind, which, on its wings,
From her to the guardian of the sky,
Bore her melancholy cry,
Bore her tender tears. She spake
As if her fond heart would break:
One while, in a sad, sweet note,
Gurgled from her straining throat,
She enforced her piteous tale,
Mournful prayer, and plaintive wail;
One while, with the shrill dispute
Quite outwearied, she was mute;
Then afresh, for her dear brood,
Her harmonious shrieks renewed.
Now she winged it round and round;
Now she skimmed along the ground;
Now from bough to bough, in haste,
The delighted robber chased,
And, alighting in his path,
Seemed to say, 'twixt grief and wrath,

"Give me back, fierce rustic rude,
Give me back my pretty brood!"
And I saw the rustic still
Answered "That, I never will!"

ESTEVAN MANUEL DE VILLEGAS. (Spanish.)
Translation of THOMAS ROSCOE.

TO THE HUMBLEBEE.

BURLY, dozing, humblebee!
Where thou art is clime for me;
Let them sail for Porto. Rique,
Far-off heats through seas to seek.
I will follow thee alone,
Thou animated torrid zone!
Zigzag steerer, desert cheerer,
Let me chase thy waving lines;
Keep me nearer, me thy hearer,
Singing over shrubs and vines.

Flower-bells,
Honeyed cells:
These the tents
Which he frequents.

Insect lover of the sun,
Joy of thy dominion!
Sailor of the atmosphere,
Swimmer through the waves of air,

Voyager of light and noon,
Epicurean of June!
Wait, I prithee, till I come
Within ear-shot of thy hum;
All without is martyrdom.

When the south wind, in May days,
With a net of shining haze
Silvers the horizon wall,
And, with softness touching all,
Tints the human countenance
With a color of romance,
And, infusing subtile heats,
Turns the sod to violets:
Thou, in sunny solitudes,
Rover of the underwoods,
The green silence dost displace
With thy mellow, breezy bass.

Hot Midsummer's petted crone!
Sweet to me thy drowsy tone,
Telling of countless sunny hours,
Long days, and solid banks of flowers;
Of gulfs of sweetness without bound,
In Indian wildernesses found;
Of Syrian peace, immortal leisure,
Firmest cheer, and birdlike pleasure.

Aught unsavory or unclean
Hath my insect never seen;

But violets, and bilberry-bells,
Maple sap, and daffodels,
Clover, catchfly, adder's-tongue,
And brier-roses, dwelt among:
All beside was unknown waste,
All was picture as he passed.

Wiser far than human seer,
Yellow-breeched philosopher!
Seeing only what is fair,
   Sipping only what is sweet,
Thou dost mock at fate and care,
   Leave the chaff and take the wheat.
When the fierce northwestern blast
Cools sea and land so far and fast,
Thou already slumberest deep;
Woe and want thou canst outsleep;
Want and woe, which torture us,
Thy sleep makes ridiculous.

RALPH WALDO EMERSON

F

OF A' THE AIRTS THE WIND CAN BLAW.

OF a' the airts the wind can blaw
  I dearly like the west;
For there the bonnie lassie lives,
  The lassie I lo'e best.
There wildwoods grow, and rivers row,
  And monie a hill between;
But day and night my fancy's flight
  Is ever wi' my Jean.

I see her in the dewy flowers,
  I see her sweet and fair;
I hear her in the tunefu' birds,
  I hear her charm the air;
There's not a bonnie flower that springs
  By fountain, shaw, or green,
There's not a bonnie bird that sings,
  But minds me o' my Jean.

ROBERT BURNS.

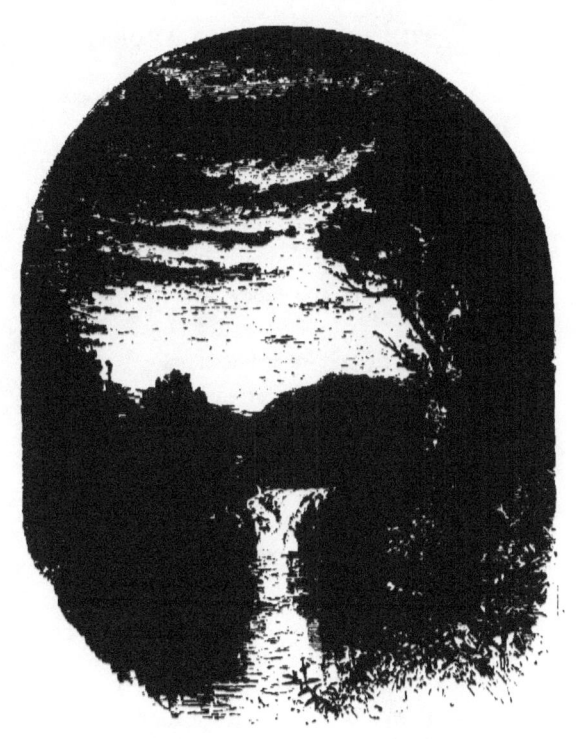

EVENING.

SWEET after showers, ambrosial air,
  That rollest from the gorgeous gloom
  Of evening, over brake and bloom
And meadow, slowly breathing bare

The round of space, and rapt below,
  Through all the dewy-tasselled wood,

67

And shadowing down the horned flood
In ripples — fan my brows, and blow

The fever from my cheek, and sigh
  The full new life that feeds thy breath
  Throughout my frame, till Doubt and Death,
Ill brethren, let the fancy fly

From belt to belt of crimson seas,
  On leagues of odor streaming far,
  To where, in yonder orient star,
A hundred spirits whisper " Peace ! "

                                ALFRED TENNYSON.

THE RIVER-GOD TO AMORET.

I AM this fountain's god. Below,
My waters to a river grow ;
And 'twixt two banks, with osiers set,
That only prosper in the wet,
Through the meadows do they glide,
Wheeling still on every side —
Sometimes winding round about,
To find the evenest channel out.
And if thou wilt go with me,
Leaving mortal company,
In the cool streams shalt thou lie,
Free from harm as well as I.
I will give thee, for thy food,
No fish that useth in the mud ;

But trout and pike, that love to swim
Where the gravel, from the brim,
Through the pure streams may be seen.
Orient pearls, fit for a queen,
Will I give, thy love to win,
And a shell to keep them in.
Not a fish in all my brook
That shall disobey thy look,
But, when thou wilt, come sliding by,
And from thy white hand take a fly.
And to make thee understand
How I can my waves command,
They shall bubble whilst I sing,
Sweeter than the silver string:

THE SONG.

Do not fear to put thy feet
Naked in the river, sweet.
Think not leech, or newt, or toad,
Will bite thy foot when thou hast trod,
Nor let the water rising high,
As thou wad'st in, make thee cry
And sob; but ever live with me,
And not a wave shall trouble thee!

JOHN FLETCHER.

SUMMER LONGINGS.

Las mañanas floridas
De Abril y Mayo.

CALDERON.

AH! my heart is weary waiting,
  Waiting for the May,
Waiting for the pleasant rambles,
Where the fragrant hawthorn brambles,
  With the woodbine alternating,
    Scent the dewy way.
  Ah! my heart is weary waiting,
    Waiting for the May.

  Ah! my heart is sick with longing,
    Longing for the May,
Longing to escape from study,
To the young face fair and ruddy,
  And the thousand charms belonging
    To the Summer's day.
  Ah! my heart is sick with longing,
    Longing for the May.

  Ah! my heart is sore with sighing,
    Sighing for the May,
Sighing for their sure returning,
When the summer beams are burning:

Hopes and flowers that, dead or dying,
  All the Winter lay.
Ah! my heart is sore with sighing,
  Sighing for the May.

Ah! my heart is pained with throbbing,
  Throbbing for the May,
Throbbing for the seaside billows,
Or the water-wooing willows,
  Where, in laughing and in sobbing,
  Glide the streams away.
Ah! my heart, my heart is throbbing,
  Throbbing for the May.

Waiting sad, dejected, weary,
  Waiting for the May!
Spring goes by with wasted warnings,
Moonlit evenings, sunbright mornings;
  Summer comes — yet dark and dreary
  Life still ebbs away.
Man is ever weary, weary,
  Waiting for the May!

                DENIS FLORENCE McCARTHY.

LINES TO AN INDIAN AIR.

I ARISE from dreams of thee
In the first sweet sleep of night,
When the winds are breathing low,
And the stars are shining bright.
I arise from dreams of thee,
And a spirit in my feet

 Has led me—who knows
  how ?
 To thy chamber window,
  sweet !

 The wandering airs, they
  faint
 On the dark and silent
  stream ;

The champak odors fail
Like sweet thoughts in a dream ;
The nightingale's complaint,
It dies upon her heart :
As I must on thine,
Beloved as thou art !

O, lift me from the grass!
I die, I faint, I fail!
Let thy love in kisses rain
On my lips and eyelids pale.
My cheek is cold and white, alas!
My heart beats loud and fast;
O, press it close to thine again,
Where it will break at last!

PERCY BYSSHE SHELLEY.

HOW THICK THE WILD FLOWERS BLOW ABOUT OUR FEET.

How thick the wild flowers blow about our feet,
Thick strewn and unregarded, which, if rare,
We should take note how beautiful they were,
How delicately wrought, of scent how sweet.
And mercies which on every path we meet,
Whose very commonness should win more praise,
Do for that very cause less wonder raise,
And these with slighter thankfulness we greet.
Yet pause *thou* often on life's onward way,
Pause time enough to stoop and gather one
Of these sweet wild flowers — time enough to tell
Its beauty over; this when thou hast done,
And marked it duly, then if thou canst lay
It wet with thankful tears into thy bosom, well!

RICHARD CHEVENIX TRENCH.

THE CAVE OF SILVER.

SEEK me the cave of silver!
Find me the cave of silver!
Rifle the cave of silver!
   Said Ilda to Brok the Bold:
So you may kiss me often;
So you may ring my finger;
So you may bind my true love
   In the round hoop of gold!

Bring me no skins of foxes;
Bring me no beds of cider;
Boast not your fifty vessels
   That fish in the Northern Sea;
For I would lie upon velvet,
And sail in a golden galley,
And naught but the cave of silver
   Will win my true love for thee.

Reena, the witch, hath told me
That up in the wild Lapp mountains
There lieth a cave of silver,
   Down deep in a valley-side;
So gather your lance and rifle,
And speed to the purple pastures,
And seek ye the cave of silver
   As you seek me for your bride.

74

I go, said Brok, right proudly;
I go to the purple pastures,
To seek for the cave of silver
　So long as my life shall hold;
But when the keen Lapp arrows
Are fleshed in the heart that loves you,
I'll leave my curse on the woman
　Who slaughtered Brok the Bold!

But Ilda laughed as she shifted
The Bergen scarf on her shoulder,
And pointed her small white finger
　Right up at the mountain gate;
And cried, O my gallant sailor,
You're brave enough to the fishes,
But the Lappish arrow is keener
　Than the back of the thorny skate!

The Summer passed, and the Winter
Came down from the icy ocean:
But back from the cave of silver
　Returned not Brok the Bold;
And Ilda waited and waited,
And sat at the door till sunset,
And gazed at the wild Lapp mountains
　That blackened the skies of gold.

I want not a cave of silver!
I care for no cave of silver!
O far beyond caves of silver
　I pine for my Brok the Bold!

O ye strong Norwegian gallants,
Go seek for my lovely lover,
And bring him to ring my finger
  With the round hoop of gold!

But the brave Norwegian gallants
They laughed at the cruel maiden,
And left her sitting in sorrow,
  Till her heart and her face grew old;
While she moaned of the cave of silver,
And moaned of the wild Lapp mountains,
And him who never will ring her
  With the round hoop of gold!

                              FITZ-JAMES O'BRIEN.

A DIRGE

CALL for the robin-redbreast and the wren,
Since o'er shady groves they hover,
And with leaves and flowers do cover
The friendless bodies of unburied men.
Call unto his funeral dole
The ant, the field-mouse, and the mole,
To rear him hillocks that shall keep him warm,
And (when gay tombs are robbed) sustain no harm;
But keep the wolf far thence, that's foe to men,
For with his nails he'll dig them up again.

                              JOHN WEBSTER.

MY LIFE IS LIKE THE SUMMER ROSE.

My life is like the summer rose
  That opens to the morning sky,
But, ere the shades of evening close,
  Is scattered on the ground — to die;
Yet on the rose's humble bed
The sweetest dews of night are shed,
As if she wept the waste to see.
But none shall weep a tear for me!

My life is like the autumn leaf
  That trembles in the moon's pale ray,
Its hold is frail, its date is brief:
  Restless — and soon to pass away;
Yet ere that leaf shall fall and fade
The parent tree will mourn its shade,
The winds bewail the leafless tree.
But none shall breathe a sigh for me!

My life is like the prints which feet
  Have left on Tampa's desert strand:
Soon as the rising tide shall beat,
  All trace will vanish from the sand;
Yet, as if grieving to efface
All vestige of the human race,
On that lone shore loud moans the sea,
But none, alas! shall mourn for me!

RICHARD HENRY WILDE.

THE ORPHAN'S CHRISTMAS-TREE.

An orphan boy, with weary feet,
  On Christmas Eve, alone, benighted,
Went through the town from street to
      street,
  To see the clustering candles lighted
In homes where happy children meet.

Before each house he stood, to mark
  The pleasant rooms that shone so fairly;
The tapers lighted, spark by spark,
  Till all the trees were blazing rarely;
And sad his heart was, in the dark.

He wept; he clasped his hands and cried:
    "Ah, every child to-night rejoices;
Their Christmas presents all divide;
    Around their trees, with merry voices;
But Christmas is to me denied.

"Once with my sister, hand in hand,
    At home, how did my tree delight me!
No other tapers shone so grand;
    But all forget me, none invite me,
Here, lonely, in the stranger's land.

"Will no one let me in, to share
    The light,—to take some corner nigh it?
In all these houses can't they spare
    A spot where I may sit in quiet—
A little seat among them there?

THE ORPHAN'S CHRISTMAS-TREE.

"Will no one let me in to-night?
  I will not beg for gift or token;
I only ask to see the sight
  And hear the thanks of others spoken,
And that will be my own delight."

He knocked at every door and gate;
  He rapped at window-pane and shutter;
But no one heard and bade him wait,
  Or came, the "Welcome in!" to utter:
Their ears were dull to outer fate.

Each father looked with eyes that smiled,
  Upon *his* happy children only:
Their gifts the mother's heart beguiled
  To think of them: none saw the lonely
Forgotten boy, the orphan child.

"O Christ-child, holy, kind, and dear!
  I have no father and no mother,
Nor friend save thee, to give me cheer.
  Be thou my help, there is none other,
Since all forget me, wandering here!"

The poor boy rubbed his hands so blue,
  His little hands, the frost made chilly;
His tattered clothes he closer drew
  And crouched within a corner stilly,
And prayed, and knew not what to do.

Then, suddenly, there shone a light;
  Along the street, approaching nearer
Another child, in garments white,
  Spake as he came — and clearer, dearer,
His voice made music in the night:

" I am the Christ! have thou no fear!
  I was a child in my probation,
And children unto me are near:
  I hear and heed thy supplication,
Though all the rest forget thee here.

" My saving Word to all I bear,
  And equally to each 'tis given;
I bring the promise of my care
  Here, in the street, beneath the heaven,
As well as in the chambers there.

" And here, poor boy, thy Christmas-tree
  Will I adorn, and so make glimmer
Through all this open space, for thee,
  That those within shall twinkle dimmer,
For bright as thine they cannot be! "

The Christ-child with his shining hand
  Then pointed up, and lo! the lustres
That sparkled there! He saw it stand,
  A tree, o'erhung with starry clusters
On all its branches, wide and grand.

So far and yet so near! the night
   Was blazing with the tapers' splendor:
What was the orphan boy's delight,
   How beat his bosom warm and tender,
To see his Christmas-tree so bright!

It seemed to him a happy dream;
   Then, from the starry branches bending,
The angels stooped, and through the gleam
   They lifted him to peace unending,
They folded him in love supreme.

The orphan child is now at rest:
   No father's care he needs, nor mother's,
Upon the Christ-child's holy breast.
   All that is here bestowed on others
He there forgets, where all is best.

BAYARD TAYLOR, AFTER RUECKERT.

BESIDE THE SEA.

I.

THEY walked beside the Summer sea,
  And watched the slowly dying sun;
And "O," she said, "come back to me!
  My love, my own, my only one!"
But while he kissed her fears away
  The gentle waters kissed the shore,
And, sadly whispering, seemed to say
  "He'll come no more! he'll come no more!"

II.

Alone beside the Autumn sea
  She watched the sombre death of day;
And "O," she said, "remember me!
  And love me, darling, far away!"
A cold wind swept the watery gloom,
  And, darkly whispering on the shore,
Sighed out the secret of his doom, —
  "He'll come no more! he'll come no more!"

III.

In peace beside the Winter sea
  A white grave glimmers in the moon;
And waves are fresh, and clouds are free,
  And shrill winds pipe a careless tune.
One sleeps beneath the dark blue wave,
  And one upon the lonely shore;
But joined in love, beyond the grave,
  They part no more! they part no more!

WILLIAM WINTER.

WHEN SPARROWS BUILD, AND THE LEAVES BREAK FORTH.

WHEN sparrows build, and the leaves break forth,
My old sorrow wakes and cries,

For I know there is dawn in the far, far north,
   And a scarlet sun doth rise;
Like a scarlet fleece the snow-field spreads,
   And the icy founts run free;
And the bergs begin to bow their heads,
   And plunge and sail in the sea.

O, my lost love, and my own, own love,
   And my love that loved me so!
Is there never a chink in the world above
   Where they listen for words from below?
Nay, I spoke once, and I grieved thee sore;
   I remember all that I said;
And now thou wilt hear me no more — no more
   Till the sea gives up her dead.

Thou didst set thy foot on the ship, and sail
   To the ice-fields and the snow;
Thou wert sad, for thy love did not avail,
   And the end I could not know.
How could I tell I should love thee to-day,
   Whom that day I held not dear?
How could I know I should love thee away
   When I did not love thee anear.

We shall walk no more through the sodden plain
   With the faded bents o'erspread;
We shall stand no more by the seething main
   While the dark wrack drives o'erhead;
We shall part no more in the wind and rain,
   Where thy last farewell was said;

FULFILMENT.

But perhaps I shall meet thee and know thee again
  When the sea gives up her dead.

JEAN INGELOW.

FULFILMENT.

WAKING in May, the peach-tree thought:
"Idle and bare! and weaving naught!
Here have I slept the winter through,
I, with my Master's work to do!"

Started the buds. The blossoms came
Till all the branches were aflame.
She rocked the birds and wove the green,
A busy tree as ever was seen -

Busy and blithe. She drank the dew,
She caught the sunbeams gliding through;
She drew her wealth from sky and soil,
And rustled gayly in her toil.

Now see the peach-tree's drooping head,
With all her fruit a-blushing red.
Knowing her Master's work is done,
She meekly resteth in the sun.

MARY ELIZABETH DODGE.

BLOW, BLOW, THOU WINTER WIND.

Blow, blow, thou winter wind!
Thou art not so unkind
    As man's ingratitude;
Thy tooth is not so keen,
Because thou art not seen,
    Although thy breath be rude.
Heigh ho! sing heigh ho! unto the green holly:
Most friendship is feigning, most loving mere folly.
    Then, heigh ho! the holly!
    This life is most jolly.

Freeze, freeze, thou bitter sky,
Thou dost not bite so nigh
    As benefits forgot;
Though thou the waters warp,
Thy sting is not so sharp
    As friend remembered not.
Heigh ho! sing heigh ho! unto the green holly:
Most friendship is feigning, most loving mere folly.
    Then, heigh ho! the holly!
    This life is most jolly.

SHAKESPEARE.

THE ROSE.

Go, lovely rose !
Tell her that wastes her time and me,
That now she knows,
When I resemble her to thee,
How sweet and fair she seems to be.

Tell her that's young,
And shuns to have her graces spied,
That hadst thou sprung
In deserts, where no men abide,
Thou must have uncommended died.

Small is the worth
Of beauty from the light retired ;
Bid her come forth,
Suffer herself to be desired,
And not blush so to be admired.

Then die — that she
The common fate of all things rare
May read in thee :
How small a part of time they share
That are so wondrous sweet and fair.

EDMUND WALLER.

A DEAD ROSE.

O ROSE! who dares to name thee?
No longer roseate now, nor soft, nor sweet;
But barren and hard, and dry as stubble-wheat:
Kept seven years in a drawer, thy titles shame thee.

The breeze that used to blow thee
Between the hedgerow thorns, and take away
An odor up the lane, to last all day,
If breathing now, unsweetened would forego thee.

The sun that used to smite thee,
And mix his glory in thy gorgeous urn,
Till beam appeared to bloom and flower to burn,
If shining now, with not a hue would light thee.

The dew that used to wet thee,
And, white first, grew incarnadined, because
It lay upon thee where the crimson was,
If dropping now, would darken where it met thee.

The fly that lit upon thee
To stretch the tendrils of its tiny feet
Along the leaf's pure edges after heat,
If lighting now, would coldly overrun thee.

89

The bee that once did suck thee,
And build thy perfumed ambers up his hive,
And swoon in thee for joy, till scarce alive,
If passing now, would blindly overlook thee.

The heart doth recognize thee,
Alone, alone! The heart doth smell thee sweet,
Doth view thee fair, doth judge thee most complete,
Though seeing now these changes that disguise thee.

Yes, and the heart doth owe thee
More love, dead rose, than to such roses bold
As Julia wears at dances, smiling cold.
Lie still upon this heart, which breaks below thee!

ELIZABETH BARRETT BROWNING.

———◆———

THE TIGER.

TIGER, Tiger, burning bright
In the forests of the night,
What immortal hand or eye
Framed thy fearful symmetry?

In what distant deeps or skies
Burned that fire within thine eyes?

On what wings dared he aspire?
What the hand dare seize the fire?

And what shoulder, and what art,
Could twist the sinews of thy heart?
When thy heart began to beat,
What dread hand formed thy dread feet?

What the hammer, what the chain,
Knit thy strength and forged thy brain?
What the anvil? What dread grasp
Dare thy deadly terrors clasp?

When the stars threw down their spears,
And water'd heaven with their tears,
Did He smile his work to see?
Did He who made the lamb make thee?

WILLIAM BLAKE.

———◆———

MY RIVER.

RIVER! my River, in the young sunshine!
   Oh, clasp afresh in thine embrace
This longing, burning frame of mine,
   And kiss my breast, and kiss my face!

So, there! — Ha, ha! — already in thine arms,
     I feel thy love, I shout, I shiver!
     But thou out-laughest loud a flouting song, proud River:
And now again my bosom warms.

The droplets of the golden sun-light glide
     Over and off me, sparkling, as I swim
Hither and thither down thy mellow tide,
     Or loll amid its crypts with outstretched limb.
I fling abroad mine arms, and lo!
     Thy wanton waves curl slyly round me;
     But ere their loose chains have well bound me,
Again they burst away, and let me go.

O sun-loved River! wherefore dost thou hum,
     Hum, hum alway, thy strange, deep, mystic song
Unto the rocks and strands? — for they are dumb,
     And answer nothing as thou flowest along.
Why singest so, all hours of night and day?
     Ah, River! my best River! thou, I guess, art seeking
     Some land where souls have still the gift of speaking
With Nature, in her own old, wondrous way.

Lo! highest heaven looms far below me here;
     I see it in thy waters, as they roll:
So beautiful, so blue, so clear —
     'T would seem, O River mine, to be thy very soul!
Oh! could I hence dive down to such a sky,
     Might I but bathe my spirit in that glory,
     So far out-shining all in ancient fairy story,
I would, indeed, have joy to die.

What, on cold earth, is deep as thou ? Is aught?
    Love is as deep, Love only is as deep.
Love lavisheth all; yet loseth, lacketh, naught.
    Like thee, too, Love can neither pause nor sleep.
Roll on, thou loving River, then ! Lift up
    Thy waves — those eyes, bright with a riotous laughing !
    Thou makest me immortal. I am quaffing
The wine of rapture from no earthly cup.

At last thou bearest me, with soothing tone,
    Back to thy bank of rosy flowers :
Thanks then, and fare thee well ! — enjoy thy bliss alone ;
    And through the year's melodious hours
Echo forever, from thy bosom broad,
    All glorious tales that sun and moon be telling;
    And woo down to their soundless fountain-dwelling
The holy stars of God !

                  EDUARD MOERIKE (German).
Translation of JAMES CLARENCE MANGAN.

SONG OF THE BROOK.

I COME from haunts of coot and hern ;
   I make a sudden sally,
And sparkle out among the fern,
   To bicker down a valley.

By thirty hills I hurry down,
 Or slip between the ridges:
By twenty thorps, a little town,
 And half a hundred bridges.

Till last by Philip's farm I flow,
 To join the brimming river;
For men may come and men may go,
 But I go on forever.

I chatter over stony ways,
 In little sharps and trebles;
I bubble into eddying bays,
 I babble on the pebbles.

With many a curve my banks I fret,
 By many a field and fallow,
And many a fairy foreland set
 With willow-weed and mallow.

I chatter, chatter, as I flow
 To join the brimming river;
For men may come and men may go,
 But I go on forever.

I wind about, and in and out,
 With here a blossom sailing,
And here and there a lusty trout,
 And here and there a grayling,

And here and there a foamy flake
    Upon me, as I travel,
With many a silvery waterbreak
    Above the golden gravel;

And draw them all along, and flow
    To join the brimming river:
For men may come and men may go,
    But I go on forever.

I steal by lawns and grassy plots;
    I slide by hazel covers;

I move the sweet forget-me-nots
 That grow for happy lovers.

I slip, I slide, I gloom, I glance,
 Among my skimming swallows .
I make the netted sunbeam dance
 Against my sandy shallows.

I murmur under moon and stars
 In brambly wildernesses ;
I linger by my shingly bars ;
 I loiter round my cresses.

And out again I curve and flow,
 To join the brimming river ;
For men may come and men may go,
 But I go on forever.

ALFRED TENNYSON

THE CALL.

AWAKE thee, my lady-love,
 Wake thee and rise !
The sun through the bower peeps
 Into thine eyes !

Behold how the early lark
 Springs from the corn !
Hark, hark ! how the flower-bird
 Winds her wee horn !

THE SEA.

The swallow's glad shriek is heard
　　All through the air;
The stock-dove is murmuring,
　　Loud as she dare.

Apollo's winged bugleman
　　Cannot contain,
But peals his loud trumpet-call
　　Once and again!

Then wake thee, my lady-love —
　　Bird of my bower!
The sweetest and sleepiest
　　Bird at this hour!

GEORGE DARLY.

THE SEA.

THROUGH the night, through the night,
　　In the saddest unrest,
Wrapt in white, all in white,
　　With her babe on her breast,
Walks the mother so pale,
Staring out on the gale
　　Through the night!

Through the night, through the night,
  Where the sea lifts the wreck,
Land in sight, close in sight!
  On the surf-flooded deck
Stands the father so brave,
Driving on to his grave
  Through the night!

                    RICHARD HENRY STODDARD.

———•———

MIDSUMMER.

THE Summer floats on even wing,
  Nor sails more far, nor draws more near;
Poised calm between the budding spring,
  And sweet decadence of the year.

In shadowed fields the cattle stand,
  The dreaming river scarcely flows,
The sky hangs cloudless o'er the land,
  And nothing comes and nothing goes.

A pause of fullness set between
  The sowing and the reaping time;
What is to be and what has been
  Joined each to each in perfect rhyme.

DIRGE.

So comes high noon 'twixt morn and eve,
  So comes full tide 'twixt ebb and flow,
Or midnight 'twixt the day we leave
  And that new day to which we go.

Full, fruitful hours by growing won,
  A restful space 'mid old and new ;
When all there was to do is done,
  And nothing yet there is to do.

No days like these so deeply blest,
  That look nor backward nor before ;
Their large fulfilment, ample rest,
  Make life flow wider evermore.

LOUISA BUSHNELL.

———◆———

DIRGE.

IF thou wilt ease thine heart
Of love, and all its smart —
  Then sleep, dear, sleep !
And not a sorrow
Hang any tear on your eyelashes.
  Lie still and deep,
Sad soul, until the sea-wave washes
The rim o' the sun to-morrow,
  In eastern sky.

But wilt thou cure thine heart
Of love, and all its smart —
   Then die, dear, die!
'T is deeper, sweeter,
  Than on a rose-bank to lie dreaming
   With folded eye;
  And then alone, amid the beaming
Of Love's stars, thou 'lt meet her
   In eastern sky.

                THOMAS LOVELL BEDDOES,

DRIFTING.

   MY soul to-day
   Is far away,
Sailing the Vesuvian Bay;
   My winged boat,
   A bird afloat,
Swims round the purple peaks remote:

   Round purple peaks
   It sails, and seeks
Blue inlets and their crystal creeks,
   Where high rocks throw,
   Through deeps below,
A duplicated golden glow.

DRIFTING.

Far, vague, and dim,
The mountains swim ;
While on Vesuvius' misty brim.
With outstretched hands
The gray smoke stands,
O'erlooking the volcanic lands.

Here Ischia smiles
O'er liquid miles ;
And yonder, bluest of the isles.
Calm Capri waits,
Her sapphire gates
Beguiling to her bright estates.

I heed not if
My rippling skiff
Float swift or slow from cliff to cliff:
With dreamful eyes
My spirit lies
Under the walls of Paradise.

Under the walls
Where swells and falls
The bay's deep breast at intervals,
At peace I lie,
Blown softly by,
A cloud upon this liquid sky.

The day, so mild,
Is Heaven's own child,
With Earth and Ocean reconciled ;

The airs I feel
Around me steal
Are murmuring to the murmuring keel.

Over the rail
My hand I trail
Within the shadow of the sail:
A joy intense,
The cooling sense
Glides down my drowsy indolence.

With dreamful eyes
My spirit lies
Where Summer sings and never dies;
O'erveiled with vines,
She glows and shines
Among her future oil and wines.

Her children, hid
The cliffs amid,
Are gambolling with the gambolling kid,
Or down the walls,
With tipsy calls,
Laugh on the rocks like waterfalls.

The fisher's child,
With tresses wild,
Unto the smooth, bright sand beguiled,
With glowing lips
Sings as she skips,
Or gazes at the far-off ships.

Yon deep bark goes
Where Traffic blows,
From lands of sun to lands of snows ,
This happier one,
Its course is run —
From lands of snow to lands of sun.

O happy ship,
To rise and dip,
With the blue crystal at your lip !
O happy crew,
My heart with you
Sails, and sails, and sings anew !

No more, no more
The worldly shore
Upbraids me with its loud uproar !
With dreamful eyes
My spirit lies
Under the walls of Paradise !

THOMAS BUCHANAN READ

THE MINSTREL'S SONG IN ELLA.

O, sing unto my roundelay!
  O, drop the briny tear with me!
Dance no more at holiday:
  Like a running river be!
     My love is dead,
     Gone to his death-bed,
     All under the willow tree.

Black his hair as the winter night,
  White his neck as the summer snow,
Ruddy his face as the morning light;
  Cold he lies in the grave below.

Sweet his tongue as the throstle's note;
  Quick in dance as thought can be:
Deft his tabor, cudgel stote.
  O! he lies by the willow tree.

Hark! the raven flaps his wing,
  In the briered dell below;
Hark! the death-owl loud doth sing
  To the nightmares as they go.

105

See! the white moon shines on high!
  Whiter is my true-love's shroud —
Whiter than the morning sky,
  Whiter than the evening cloud.

Here, upon my true-love's grave,
  Shall the gairish flowers be laid;
Nor one holy saint to save
  All the sorrows of a maid.

With my hands I'll bind the briers,
  Round his holy corse to gre;
Elf and fairy, light your fires!
  Here my body still shall be.

Come, with acorn-cup and thorn!
  Drain my heart's blood all away!
Life and all its good I scorn:
  Dance by night, or feast by day!
     My love is dead,
     Gone to his death-bed,
     All under the willow tree.

Water-witches, crowned with reytes,
  Bear me to your deadly tide!
I die! — I come! My true-love waits!
  Thus the damsel spake — and died.

THOMAS CHATTERTON.

QUA CURSUM VENTUS.

As ships becalmed at eve, that lay
  With canvas drooping, side by side,
Two towers of sail, at dawn of day
  Are scarce long leagues apart descried :

When fell the night, up-sprung the breeze,
  And all the darkling hours they plied ;
Nor dreamt but each the self-same seas
  By each was cleaving, side by side :

E'en so — but why the tale reveal
    Of those whom, year by year unchanged,
Brief absence joined anew, to feel,
    Astounded, soul from soul estranged?

At dead of night their sails were filled,
    And onward each rejoicing steered;
Ah! neither blame, for neither willed
    Or wist what first with dawn appeared.

To veer, how vain! On, onward strain,
    Brave barks! — in light, in darkness too!
Through winds and tides one compass guides:
    To that and your own selves be true.

But O blithe breeze! and O great seas!
    Though ne'er that earliest parting past,
On your wide plain they join again;
    Together lead them home at last.

One port, methought, alike they sought —
    One purpose hold where'er they fare;
O bounding breeze, O rushing seas,
    At last, at last, unite them there!

ARTHUR HUGH CLOUGH

AS I LAY A-THINKING.

As I lay a-thinking, a-thinking, a-thinking,
  Merry sang the Bird as she sat upon the spray:
      There came a noble Knight
      With his hauberk shining bright,
      And his gallant heart was light —
          Free and gay;
  And as I lay a-thinking, he rode upon his way.

As I lay a-thinking, a-thinking, a-thinking,
  Sadly sang the Bird as she sat upon the tree:
      There seemed a crimson plain,
      Where a gallant Knight lay slain,
      And a steed with broken rein
          Ran free:
  As I lay a-thinking — most pitiful to see!

As I lay a-thinking, a-thinking, a-thinking,
  Merry sang the Bird as she sat upon the bough:
      A lovely Maid came by,
      And a gentle Youth was nigh,
      And he breathed many a sigh,
          And a vow;
  As I lay a-thinking — her heart was gladsome now.

As I lay a-thinking, a-thinking, a-thinking,
  Sadly sang the Bird as she sat upon the thorn:
      No more a Youth was there,
      But a Maiden rent her hair,

And cried in sad despair,
      "That I was born!"
As I lay a-thinking, she perishèd forlorn.

As I lay a-thinking, a-thinking, a-thinking,
  Sweetly sang the Bird as she sat upon the brier:
      There came a lovely Child,
      And his face was meek and mild,
      Yet joyously he smiled
            On his sire:
As I lay a-thinking — a cherub might admire.

But as I lay a-thinking, a-thinking, a-thinking,
  And sadly sang the Bird as it perched upon a bier,
      That joyous smile was gone,
      And the face was white and wan,
      As the down upon the swan
            Doth appear:
As I lay a-thinking, oh! bitter flowed the tear!

As I lay a-thinking, the golden sun was sinking —
  Oh! merry sang that Bird as it glittered on her breast
      With a thousand gorgeous dyes,
      While, soaring to the skies,
      'Mid the stars she seemed to rise,
            As to her nest.
As I lay a-thinking, her meaning was exprest:
      " Follow, follow me away!
      It boots not to delay:"
      ('T was so she seemed to say)
            " Here is rest!"

RICHARD HARRIS BARHAM

TO CYNTHIA.

Queen and huntress, chaste and fair,
  Now the sun is laid to sleep,
Seated in thy silver chair,
  State in wonted manner keep:
Hesperus entreats thy light,
Goddess excellently bright!

Earth, let not thy envious shade
  Dare itself to interpose;
Cynthia's shining orb was made
  Heaven to clear when day did close:
Bless us, then, with wished sight,
Goddess excellently bright!

Lay thy bow of pearl apart,
  And thy crystal-shining quiver;
Give unto thy flying hart
  Space to breathe, how short soever:
Thou that makest a day of night,
Goddess excellently bright!

                              Ben Jonson.

111

TO THE GRASSHOPPER AND CRICKET.

GREEN little vaulter in the sunny grass,
Catching your heart up at the feel of June!
Sole voice that's heard amidst the lazy noon,
When even the bees lag at the summoning brass!
And you, warm little housekeeper, who class
With those who think the candles come too soon,
Loving the fire, and with your tricksome tune
Nick the glad silent moments as they pass!

O sweet and tiny cousins! that belong,
One to the fields, the other to the hearth!
Both have your sunshine; both, though small, are strong
At your clear hearts; and both seem given to earth
To sing in thoughtful ears this natural song —
In doors and out, summer and winter, mirth!

LEIGH HUNT.

PASSING THE ICEBERGS.

A FEARLESS shape of brave device,
  Our vessel drives through mist and rain,
Between the floating fleets of ice —
  The navies of the northern main.

These Arctic ventures, blindly hurled,
  The proofs of Nature's olden force,
Like fragments of a crystal world
  Long shattered from its skyey course —

These are the buccaneers that fright
  The middle sea with dream of wrecks,
And freeze the south winds in their flight,
  And chain the Gulf-stream to their decks.

At every dragon prow and helm
  There stands some Viking, as of yore :
Grim heroes from the boreal realm
  Where Odin rules the spectral shore.

And oft beneath the sun or moon
  Their swift and eager falchions glow,
While, like a storm-vexed wind, the rune
  Comes chafing through some beard of snow.

And when the far North flashes up,
  With fires of mingled red and gold,
They know that many a blazing cup
  Is brimming to the absent bold.

Up signal there ! and let us hail
  Yon looming phantom as we pass !
Note all her fashion, hull and sail,
  Within the compass of your glass.

II

See at her mast the steadfast glow
  Of that one star of Odin's throne:
Up with our flag! and let us show
  The constellation on our own.

And speak her well; for she might say,
  If from her heart the words could thaw,
Great news from some far frozen bay,
  Or the remotest Esquimaux:

Might tell of channels yet untold,
  That sweep the pole from sea to sea;

Of lands which God designs to hold
  A mighty people yet to be;

Of wonders which alone prevail
  Where day and darkness dimly meet;
Of all which spreads the Arctic sail;
  Of Franklin, and his venturous fleet:

How, haply, at some glorious goal
  His anchor holds, his sails are furled;
That Fame has named him on her scroll
  " Columbus of the Polar world!"

Or how his ploughing barks wedge on
  Through splintering fields, with battered shares,
Lit only by that spectral dawn,
  The mask that mocking darkness wears;

Or how, o'er embers black and few,
  The last of shivered masts and spars,
He sits amid his frozen crew,
  In council with the norland stars.

No answer — but the sullen flow
  Of ocean, heaving long and vast;
An argosy of ice and snow,
  The voiceless North swings proudly past.

THOMAS BUCHANAN READ

THE ANGLER'S WISH.

I in these flowery meads would be :
These crystal streams should solace me,
To whose harmonious, bubbling noise
I with my angle would rejoice —
    Sit here and see the turtle-dove
    Court his chaste mate to acts of love.

Or on that bank, feel the west wind
Breathe health and plenty ; please my mind

To see sweet dew-drops kiss these flowers,
And then washed off by April showers;
    Here hear my Kenna sing a song,
    There see a blackbird feed her young,

Or a leverock build her nest;
Here give my weary spirits rest,
And raise my low-pitched thoughts above
Earth, or what poor mortals love:
    Thus, free from lawsuits, and the noise
    Of princes' courts, I would rejoice.

Or, with my Bryan and a book,
Loiter long days near Shawford brook.
There sit by him, and eat my meat;
There see the sun both rise and set;
There bid good morning to next day;
There meditate my time away;
    And angle on; and beg to have
    A quiet passage to a welcome grave.

ISAAK WALTON

TO THE NIGHTINGALE.

O NIGHTINGALE, that on yon bloomy spray
    Warblest at eve, when all the woods are still!
    Thou with fresh hope the lover's heart dost fill,
While the jolly hours lead on propitious May.

Thy liquid notes that close the eye of day,
    First heard before the shallow cuckoo's bill,
    Portend success in love. O, if Jove's will
Have linked that amorous power to thy soft lay,
    Now timely sing, ere the rude bird of hate
Foretell my hopeless doom in some grove nigh ;
    As thou from year to year hast sung too late
For my relief, yet hadst no reason why.
    Whether the Muse or Love call thee his mate,
    Both them I serve, and of their train am I.

JOHN MILTON.

THE DWINA.

STONY-BROWED Dwina, thy face is as flint !
Horsemen and wagons cross, scoring no dint ;
Cossacks patrol thee, and leave thee as hard ;
Camp-fires but blacken and spot thee, like pard ,
        For the dead, silent river lies rigid and still.

Down on thy sedgy banks picket the troops,
Scaring the night-wolves with carols and whoops ;
Crackle their fagots of drift-wood and hay,
And the steam of their pots fills the nostrils of day ;
        But the dead, silent river lies rigid and still.

Sledges pass sliding from hamlet to town :
Lovers and comrades — and none doth he drown !

Harness-bells tinkling in musical glee,
For to none comes the sorrow that came unto me ;
  And the dead, silent river lies rigid and still.

I go to the Dwina ; I stand on his wave,
Where Ivan, my dead, has no grass on his grave :
Stronger than granite that coffins a Czar,
Solid as pavement, and polished as spar —
  Where the dead, silent river lies rigid and still.

Stronger than granite ? Nay, falser than sand !
Fatal the clasp of thy slippery hand ;
Cruel as vulture's the clutch of thy claws ;
Who shall redeem from the merciless jaws
  Of the dead, silent river, so rigid and still ?

Crisp lay the new-fallen snow on thy breast,
Trembled the white moon through haze in the west ;
Far in the thicket the wolf-cub was howling,
Down by the sheep-cotes the wolf-dam was prowling ;
  And the dead, silent river lay rigid and still :

When Ivan, my lover, my husband, my lord,
Lightly and cheerily stept on the sward —
Light with his hopes of the morrow and me,
That the reeds on the margin leaned after to see ;
  But the dead, silent river lay rigid and still.

O'er the fresh snow-fall, the winter-long frost,
O'er the broad Dwina the forester crost :

Snares at his girdle, and gun at his side,
Game-bag weighed heavy with gifts for his bride;
    And the dead, silent river lay rigid and still —

Rigid and silent, and crouching for prey,
Crouching for him who went singing his way.
Oxen were stabled, and sheep were in fold;
But Ivan was struggling in torrents ice-cold,
    'Neath the dead, silent river, so rigid and still.

Home he came never. We searched by the ford:
Small was the fissure that swallowed my lord;
Glassy ice-sheetings had frozen above —
A crystalline cover to seal up my love,
    In the dead, silent river, so rigid and still.

Still by the Dwina my home-torches burn;
Faithful I watch for my bridegroom's return.
When the moon sparkles on hoar-frost and tree,
I see my love crossing the Dwina to me,
    O'er the dead, silent river, so rigid and still.

Always approaching, he never arrives.
Howls the northeast wind, the dusty snow drives.
Snapping like touchwood, I hear the ice crack —
And my lover is drowned in the water-hole black,
    'Neath the dead, silent river, so rigid and still.

                COUNTESS ORLOFF. (Russian.)
Translation of MRS. OGILVIE.

THE KNIGHT'S TOMB.

WHERE is the grave of Sir Arthur O'Kellyn?
        Where may the grave of that good man be?
By the side of a spring on the breast of Helvellyn,
        Under the twigs of a young birch-tree.
The oak that in summer was sweet to hear,
And rustled its leaves in the fall of the year,
And whistled and roared in the winter alone,
Is gone, and the birch in its stead has grown.

The knight's bones are dust,
And his good sword rust;
His soul is with the saints, I trust.

SAMUEL TAYLOR COLERIDGE.

KULNASATZ, MY REINDEER.

KULNASATZ, my reindeer,
We have a long journey to go;
    The moors are vast,
    And we must haste,
Our strength, I fear,
Will fail if we are slow:
        And so
    Our songs will, too.

Kaigè, the watery moor,
Is pleasant unto me,
    Though long it be,
Since it doth to my mistress lead
    Whom I adore;
    The Kilwa moor
I ne'er again will tread.

Thoughts filled my mind,
Whilst I through Kaigè passed
    Swift as the wind,

And my desire
Winged with impatient fire :
My reindeer, let us haste !

So shall we quickly end our pleasing pain —
Behold my mistress there,
With decent motion walking o'er the plain !
Kulnasatz, my reindeer,
Look yonder ! where
She washes in the lake !
See ! while she swims,
The water from her purer limbs
New clearness take !

ANONYMOUS. (Icelandic.)

Anonymous Translation.

THE ROSEBUD.

WHEN Nature tries her finest touch,
' Weaving her vernal wreath,
Mark ye how close she veils her round,
Not to be traced by sight or sound,
Nor soiled by ruder breath ?

Who ever saw the earliest rose
First open her sweet breast ?
Or, when the summer sun goes down,
The first soft star in evening's crown
Light up her gleaming crest ?

Fondly we seek the dawning bloom
    On features wan and fair:
The gazing eye no change can trace;
But look away a little space —
    Then turn — and lo! 't is there.

But there 's a sweeter flower than e'er
    Blushed on the rosy spray,
A brighter star, a richer bloom,
Than e'er did western heaven illume
    At close of summer day.

'T is love, the last best gift of Heaven —
    Love, gentle, holy, pure!
But, tenderer than a dove's soft eye,
The searching sun, the open sky,
    She never could endure.

Even human love will shrink from sight,
    Here in the coarse rude earth:
How then should rash intruding glance
Break in upon her sacred trance
    Who boasts a heavenly birth?

So still and secret is her growth,
    Ever the truest heart,
Where deepest strikes her kindly root,
For hope or joy, for flower or fruit,
    Least knows its happy part.

God only, and good angels, look
    Behind the blissful screen —
As when, triumphant o'er His woes,
The Son of God by moonlight rose,
    By all but heaven unseen :

As when the holy Maid beheld
    Her risen Son and Lord ;
Thought hath not colors half so fair
That she to paint that hour may dare,
    In silence best adored.

The gracious Dove, that brought from heaven
    The earnest of our bliss,
Of many a chosen witness telling,
On many a happy vision dwelling,
    Sings not a note of this.

So, truest image of the Christ,
    Old Israel's long-lost son,
What time, with sweet forgiving cheer,
He called his conscious brethren near,
    Would weep with them alone :

He could not trust his melting soul
    But in his Maker's sight ;
Then why should gentle hearts and true
Bare to the rude world's withering view
    Their treasure of delight.

No! let the dainty rose awhile
     Her bashful fragrance hide;
Rend not her silken veil too soon,
But leave her in her own soft noon
     To flourish and abide.

                    JOHN KEBLE.

SONG.

TRICKLES fast the April shower,
    Like the maiden's tear,
In the tardy trysting hour,
    And no lover near.

Joy, be sure, will soon return;
    See, out-shines the sun!
Earth will bloom and cheeks will burn
    With blushes many a one.

Heaven will bless the happy glow,
    So the heart be true:
Sun and shower may flit and flow,
    Love will shine all through.

                 THE AFTERGLOW.

BOATMAN'S HYMN.

BARK, that bears me through foam and squall,
You in the storm are my castle-wall!
Though the sea should redden from bottom to top,
From tiller to mast she takes no drop.
> *On the tide top, the tide top —*
> *Wherry aroon, my land and store!*
> *On the tide top, the tide top,*
> *She is the boat can sail galore!*

She dresses herself, and goes gliding on,
Like a dame in her robes of the Indian lawn;
For God has blessed her, gunnel and wale —
And O! if you saw her stretch out to the gale,
> *On the tide top, the tide top —*
> *Wherry aroon, my land and store!*
> *On the tide top, the tide top,*
> *She is the boat can sail galore!*

Whillan ahoy! — Old heart of stone,
Stooping so black o'er the beach alone,
Answer me well: on the bursting brine
Saw you ever a bark like mine,
> *On the tide top, the tide top?*
> *Wherry aroon, my land and store!*
> *On the tide top, the tide top,*
> *She is the boat can sail galore!*

SAYS Whillan, Since first I was made of stone,
I have looked abroad o'er the beach alone;
But, till to-day, on the bursting brine,
Saw I never a bark like thine!

On the tide top, the tide top —
Wherry aroon, my land and store!
On the tide top, the tide top,
She is the boat can sail galore!

God of the air! the seamen shout,
When they see us tossing the brine about,

Give us the shelter of strand or rock,
Or through and through us she goes with a shock!
     On the tide top, the tide top —
     Wherry aroon, my land and store!
     On the tide top, the tide top,
     She is the boat can sail galore!

                        ANONYMOUS.   (Irish.)

Translation of SAMUEL FERGUSON.

UP-HILL.

DOES the road wind up-hill all the way?
    Yes, to the very end.
Will the day's journey take the whole long day?
    From morn to night, my friend.

But is there for the night a resting-place?
    A roof for when the slow dark hours begin?
May not the darkness hide it from my face?
    You cannot miss that inn.

Shall I meet other wayfarers at night?
    : Those who have gone before.
Then must I knock, or call when just in sight?
    They will not keep you standing at that door.

Shall I find comfort, travel-sore and weak?
    Of labor you shall find the sum.
Will there be beds for me and all who seek?
    Yea, beds for all who come.

CHRISTINA G. ROSSETTI.

IF ALL WERE RAIN AND NEVER SUN.

If all were rain and never sun
  No bow could span the hill;
If all were sun and never rain,
  There'd be no rainbow still.

CHRISTINA G. ROSSETTI.

WAKE, LADY!

Up! quit thy bower! late wears the hour,
Long have the rooks cawed round the tower;
O'er flower and tree loud hums the bee,
And the wild kid sports merrily.
The sun is bright, the sky is clear:
Wake, lady, wake! and hasten here.

Up! maiden fair, and bind thy hair,
And rouse thee in the breezy air!

131

The lulling stream that soothed thy dream
Is dancing in the sunny beam.
Waste not these hours, so fresh, so gay:
Leave thy soft couch, and haste away!

Up! Time will tell the morning bell
Its service-sound has chiměd well;
The aged crone keeps house alone,
The reapers to the fields are gone.
Lose not these hours, so cool, so gay:
Lo! while thou sleep'st they haste away!

JOANNA BAILLIE.

THE MERRY LARK WAS UP AND SINGING.

THE merry, merry lark was up and singing,
    And the hare was out and feeding on the lea,
And the merry, merry bells below were ringing,
    When my child's laugh rang through me.
Now the hare is snared, and dead beside the snow-yard,
    And the lark beside the dreary winter sea,
And my baby in his cradle in the churchyard
    Waiteth there until the bells bring me.

CHARLES KINGSLEY.

THE WRECK OF THE HESPERUS.

It was the schooner Hesperus
    That sailed the wintry sea;
And the skipper had taken his little daughter,
    To bear him company.

Blue were her eyes as the fairy flax,
    Her cheeks like the dawn of day,
And her bosom white as the hawthorn buds
    That ope in the month of May.

The skipper he stood beside the helm :
    His pipe was in his mouth;
And he watched how the veering flaw did blow
    The smoke — now west, now south.

Then up and spake an old sailor,
    Had sailed the Spanish main :
" I pray thee, put into yonder port;
    For I fear a hurricane.

" Last night the moon had a golden ring,
    And to-night no moon we see ! "
The skipper he blew a whiff from his pipe,
    And a scornful laugh laughed he.

Colder and louder blew the wind,
    A gale from the north-east;
The snow fell hissing in the brine,
    And the billows frothed like yeast.

Down came the storm, and smote amain
    The vessel in its strength;
She shuddered and paused, like a frighted steed,
    Then leaped her cable's length.

"Come hither, come hither! my little daughter,
    And do not tremble so;
For I can weather the roughest gale
    That ever wind did blow."

He wrapped her warm in his seaman's coat,
    Against the stinging blast;
He cut a rope from a broken spar,
    And bound her to the mast.

"O father, I hear the church-bells ring!
    O say what may it be?"
"'Tis a fog-bell on a rock-bound coast!"
    And he steered for the open sea.

"O father, I hear the sound of guns!
    O say what may it be?"
"Some ship in distress, that cannot live
    In such an angry sea!"

" O father, I see a gleaming light !
    O say what may it be ? "
But the father answered never a word :
    A frozen corpse was he.

Lashed to the helm, all stiff and stark,
    With his face turned to the skies,
The lantern gleamed through the gleaming snow
    On his fixed and glassy eyes.

Then the maiden clasped her hands and prayed,
    That saved she might be ;
And she thought of Christ, who stilled the wave
    On the Lake of Galilee.

And fast through the midnight dark and drear,
    Through the whistling sleet and snow,
Like a sheeted ghost the vessel swept,
    Towards the reef of Norman's Woe.

And ever, the fitful gusts between,
    A sound came from the land ;
It was the sound of the trampling surf
    On the rocks and the hard sea-sand.

The breakers were right beneath her bows :
    She drifted a dreary wreck ;
And a whooping billow swept the crew,
    Like icicles, from her deck.

She struck where the white and fleecy waves
    Looked soft as carded wool ;
But tho cruel rocks, they gored her side
    Like the horns of an angry bull.

Her rattling shrouds, all sheathed in ice,
    With the masts went by the board ;
Like a vessel of glass, she stove and sank :
    Ho ! ho ! the breakers roared !

At daybreak, on the bleak sea-beach,
    A fisherman stood aghast,
To see the form of a maiden fair,
    Lashed close to a drifting mast.

The salt sea was frozen on her breast,
    The salt tears in her eyes ;
And he saw her hair, like the brown sea-weed,
    On the billows fall and rise.

Such was the wreck of the Hesperus,
    In the midnight and the snow.
Christ save us all from a death like this,
    On the reef of Norman's Woe !

HENRY WADSWORTH LONGFELLOW

HE snow lies fresh on Chester Hill
    To take red Reynard's fet-locks fair ;
His scent is sure, for the wind is still
    Above the Delaware's frozen glare ; —
"Bring out yer fox-houn's, Jasper Gill,
    An' let 'em snuff the mornin' air ! "

So thundered at the cabin door
    Of grizzly Jasper in the glen,
The keenest shot on Homen's shore,
    Known miles around as Bearskin
        Ben —
Whose weather-beaten visage bore
    The tracks of fifty years and ten.

"Untie the brave old houn' whose voice
    Bays mellower than a meetin' bell;
Loose silk-ear'd Fan for me, my choice
    'Mong all the dogs in Beaver Dell ; —

137

They're a pair to make the heart rejoice
 An' bound like a buck when hunted well ! "

Gray Jasper hears his comrade call,
 And, whistling to his eager pack,
Down snatches from the cabin-wall
 His rifle, hung on stag-horn rack ;
Bids wife farewell till twilight-fall,
 And strides away on the red-fox track.

O'er mountain-crest, 'cross lowland vale,
 Where Hero hotly leads the chase,
These bluff old woodsmen press the trail,
 Close Indian-file, with tireless pace —
Till, hark ! the fox-hound's deep-toned hail
 Proclaims the game on the home-stretch race.

Athwart the brow of Chester Hill
 Scared Reynard, like a blazing sun,
Flies on before his foes until,
 O'erleaping rock and ice-bound run,
He draws the aim of Jasper Gill
 Along the barrel of his gun.

The ledges ring to the rifle's crack
 The fatal bullet whistles past !
A loud " halloo " comes echoing back
 To Bearskin Ben, on the rising blast :
A crimson stream bedyes the track ; —
 And Reynard strikes his flag at last !

" Call in the dogs! " cries Jasper Gill:
  " The sport is done, the chase is o'er ; —
I've gi'n yon thievin' skulk a pill!
  He'll rob my poultry-yard no more.
Come, Ben, let's beat to the cabin sill,
  Where the old wife waits us at the door."

Beside a roaring hickory blaze,
  With laugh and joke and rustic cheer,
These glib-tongued cronies sound the praise
  Of dog and gun in Molly's ear,
Till the old dame's needle almost plays
  A tune through her good man's hunting-gear.

                                    G. H. BARNES.

THE LOVER TO THE GLOW-WORMS.

Ye living lamps, by whose dear light
  The nightingale does sit so late,
And, studying all the summer night,
  Her matchless songs does meditate!

Ye country comets, that portend
  No war, nor prince's funeral —
Shining unto no other end
  Than to presage the grass's fall!

Ye glow-worms, whose officious flame
  To wandering mowers shows the way,
That in the night have lost their aim
  And after foolish fires do stray!

Your courteous lights in vain you waste,
  Since Juliana here is come;
For she my mind hath so displaced,
  That I shall never find my home.

ANDREW MARVELL.

THE WEE GREEN NEUK.

O the wee green neuk, the sly green neuk,
  The wee sly neuk for me!
Whare the wheat is wavin' bright and brown,
  And the wind is fresh and free:

Whare I weave wild weeds, and out o' reeds
    Kerve whissles as I lay,
And a douce low voice is murmurin' by,
    Through the lee-lang simmer day!

And whare a' things luik as though they lo'ed
    To languish in the sun,
And that if they feed the fire they dree
    They wadna ae pang were gone;
Whare the lift aboon is still as death,
    And bright as life can be;
While the douce low voice says Na, na, na!
    But ye mauna luik sae at me!

Whare the lang rank bent is saft and cule,
    And freshenin' till the feet;
And the spot is sly, and the spinnie high,
    Whare my luve and I mak seat;
And I tease her till she rins, and then
    I catch her roun' the tree,
While the poppies shak' their heids and blush:
    Let 'em blush till they drap, for me!

O the wee green neuk, the sly green neuk,
    The wee sly neuk for me!
Whare the wheat is wavin' bright and brown,
    And the wind is fresh and free!
                   PHILIP JAMES BAILEY.

God does not send us strange flowers every year.
When the spring winds blow over the pleasant place,
The same dear things lifting up the same fair faces,
The violet is here.

Adeline D.T. Whitney.

A VIOLET.

God does not send us strange flowers every year.
When the spring winds blow o'er the pleasant places,
The same dear things lift up the same fair faces.
  The violet is here.

It all comes back: the odor, grace, and hue;
Each sweet relation of its life repeated:
No blank is left, no looking-for is cheated;
  It is the thing we knew.

So after the death-winter it must be.
God will not put strange signs in the heavenly places:
The old love shall look out from the old faces.
  Veilchen! I shall have thee!

      Adeline D. T. Whitney.

THE SONGSTER.

A MIDSUMMER CAROL.

I.

Within our summer hermitage
  I have an aviary,—
'Tis but a little, rustic cage,
That holds a golden-winged Canary:
A bird with no companion of his kind.
  But when the warm south wind

143

Blows, from rathe meadows, over
The honey-scented clover,
I hang him in the porch, that he may hear
The voices of the bobolink and thrush,
The robin's joyous gush,
The bluebird's warble, and the tunes of all
Glad matin songsters in the fields anear.
Then, as the blithe responses vary,
And rise anew, and fall,
In every hush
He answers them again,
With his own wild, reliant strain,
As if he breathed the air of sweet Canary.

II.

Bird, bird of the golden wing,
Thou lithe, melodious thing !
Where hast thy music found ?
What fantasies of vale and vine,
Of glades where orchids intertwine,
Of palm-trees, garlanded and crowned,
And forests flooded deep with sound —
What high imagining
Hath made this carol thine ?
By what instinct art thou bound
To all rare harmonies that be
In those green islands of the sea,
Where thy radiant, wildwood kin
Their madrigals at morn begin,

Above the rainbow and the roar
Of the long billow from the Afric shore?
    Asking other guardon
    None, than Heaven's light,
Holding thy crested head aright,
    Thy melody's sweet burden
    Thou dost proudly utter,
With many an ecstatic flutter
And ruffle of thy tawny throat
    For each delicious note.
—Art thou a waif from Paradise,
    In some fine moment wrought
By an artist of the skies,
    Thou winged, cherubic Thought?

    Bird of the amber beak,
    Bird of the golden wing!
Thy dower is thy carolling;
    Thou hast not far to seek
    Thy bread, nor needest wine
To make thine utterance divine;
Thou art canopied and clothed
    And unto Song betrothed!
In thy lone aërial cage
Thou hast thine ancient heritage;
There is no task-work on thee laid
But to rehearse the ditties thou hast made;
    Thou hast a lordly store,
And, though thou scatterest them free,
    Art richer than before,
        Holding in fee
The glad domain of minstrelsy.

III.

Brave songster, bold Canary!
Thou art not of thy listeners wary,
Art not timorous, nor chary
  Of quaver, trill, and tone,
  Each perfect and thine own;
But renewest, shrill or soft,
Thy greeting to the upper skies,
Chanting thy latest song aloft
With no tremor nor disguise.
Thine is a music that defies
  The envious rival near;
  Thou hast no fear
Of the day's vogue, the scornful critic's sneer.

Would, O wisest bard, that now
  I could cheerly sing as thou!
Would I might chant the thoughts which on me throng,
For the very joy of song!
  Here, on the written page,
I falter, yearning to impart
The vague and wandering murmur of my heart,
Haply a little to assuage
This human restlessness and pain,
  And half forget my chain:
Thou, unconscious of thy cage,
Showerest music everywhere;
  Thou hast no care
But to pour out the largesse thou hast won
From the south wind and the sun:

There are no prison-bars
Betwixt thy tricksy spirit and the stars.

    When from its delicate clay
Thy little life shall pass away,
    Thou wilt not meanly die,
Nor voiceless yield to silence and decay ;
    But triumph still in art
    And act thy minstrel-part,
    Lifting a last, long pæan
To the unventured empyrean.
    — So bid the world go by,
    And they who list to thee aright,
Seeing thee fold thy wings and fall, shall say :
" The Songster perished of his own delight ! "

                    EDMUND CLARENCE STEDMAN.

SONG.

    COME with the birds in the spring,
        Thou whose voice rivalleth theirs ;
    Come with the flowers, and bring
        Sweet shame to their bloom unawares :

    Come, — but O, how can I wait !
        Come through the snows of to-day !
    Come, and the gray Earth elate
        Shall leap for thy sake into May !

                    HARRIET McEWEN KIMBALL.

THE BAREFOOT BOY.

BLESSINGS on thee, little man,
Barefoot boy, with cheek of tan!
With thy turned-up pantaloons,
And thy merry whistled tunes;
With thy red lip, redder still

Kissed by strawberries on the hill;
With the sunshine on thy face,
Through thy torn brim's jaunty grace!
From my heart I give thee joy:
I was once a barefoot boy.
Prince thou art — the grown-up man
Only is republican.
Let the million-dollared ride!
Barefoot, trudging at his side,
Thou hast more than he can buy,
In the reach of ear and eye:
Outward sunshine, inward joy.
Blessings on thee, barefoot boy!

O! for boyhood's painless play,
Sleep that wakes in laughing day,
Health that mocks the doctor's rules,
Knowledge never learned of schools:
Of the wild bee's morning chase,
Of the wild flower's time and place,
Flight of fowl, and habitude
Of the tenants of the wood;
How the tortoise bears his shell,
How the woodchuck digs his cell,
And the ground-mole sinks his well;
How the robin feeds her young,
How the oriole's nest is hung;
Where the whitest lilies blow,
Where the freshest berries grow,
Where the ground-nut trails its vine,
Where the wood-grape's clusters shine;

Of the black wasp's cunning way,
Mason of his walls of clay,
And the architectural plans
Of gray hornet artisans!
For, eschewing books and tasks,
Nature answers all he asks;
Hand in hand with her he walks.
Face to face with her he talks,
Part and parcel of her joy.
Blessings on the barefoot boy!

O for boyhood's time of June,
Crowding years in one brief moon,
When all things I heard or saw,
Me, their master, waited for!
I was rich in flowers and trees,
Humming-birds and honey-bees;
For my sport the squirrel played,
Plied the snouted mole his spade;
For my taste the blackberry cone
Purpled over hedge and stone;
Laughed the brook for my delight,
Through the day and through the night:
Whispering at the garden wall,
Talked with me from fall to fall;
Mine the sand-rimmed pickerel pond,
Mine the walnut slopes beyond,
Mine, on bending orchard trees,
Apples of Hesperides!
Still, as my horizon grew,
Larger grew my riches too,

All the world I saw or knew
Seemed a complex Chinese toy,
Fashioned for a barefoot boy!

O, for festal dainties spread,
Like my bowl of milk and bread,
Pewter spoon and bowl of wood,
On the door-stone, gray and rude!
O'er me, like a regal tent,
Cloudy-ribbed, the sunset bent:
Purple-curtained, fringed with gold,
Looped in many a wind-swung fold;
While, for music, came the play
Of the pied frogs' orchestra;
And, to light the noisy choir,
Lit the fly his lamp of fire.
I was monarch; pomp and joy
Waited on the barefoot boy!

Cheerily, then, my little man!
Live and laugh as boyhood can;
Though the flinty slopes be hard,
Stubble-speared the new-mown sward,
Every morn shall lead thee through
Fresh baptisms of the dew;
Every evening from thy feet
Shall the cool wind kiss the heat;
All too soon these feet must hide
In the prison-cells of pride,
Lose the freedom of the sod,
Like a colt's for work be shod,

Made to tread the mills of toil,
Up and down in ceaseless moil:
Happy if their track be found
Never on forbidden ground;
Happy if they sink not in
Quick and treacherous sands of sin.
Ah! that thou couldst know thy joy,
Ere it passes, barefoot boy!

                              JOHN GREENLEAF WHITTIER.

———◆———

THE RAILWAY RIDE.

IN their yachts on ocean gliding,
On their steeds Arabian riding,
Whirled o'er snows on tinkling sledges,
    Men forget their woe and pain;
What the pleasure then should fill them —
What the ecstasy should thrill them —
Borne with ponderous speed, and thunderous.
    O'er the narrow iron plain.

Restless as a dream of vengeance,
Mark you there the iron engines
Blowing steam from snorting nostrils,
    Moving each upon its track;
Sighing, panting, anxious, eager,
Not with purpose mean or meagre,
But intense intent for motion,
    For the liberty they lack.

Now one screams in triumph, for the
Engine-driver, grimed and swarthy,
Lays his hand upon the lever,
　　And the steed is loose once more ;
Off it moves, and fast and faster,
With no urging from the master,
Till the awed earth shakes in terror
　　At the rumbling and the roar.

Crossing long and thread-like bridges,
Spanning streams, and cleaving ridges,
Sweeping over broad green meadows,
　　That in starless darkness lay —
How the engine rocks and clatters,
Showers of fire around it scatters,

While its blazing eye outpeering
  Looks for perils in the way.

To yon tunnel-drift careering,
In its brown mouth disappearing,'
Past from sight and passed from hearing,
  Silence follows like a spell;
Then a sudden sound-burst surges,
As the train from earth emerges
With a scream of exultation,
  With a wild and joyous yell.

With the chariot swift of Ares
Which a god to battle carries?
What the steeds the rash boy handled
  Harnessed to the sun-god's wain?
Those are mythic; this is real;
Born not of the past ideal,
But of craft and strength and purpose,
  Love of speed and thirst of gain.

O! what wildness! O! what gladness!
O! what joy akin to madness!
O! what reckless feeling raises
  Us to-day beyond the stars!
What to us all human ant-hills,
Fame fools sigh for, land that man tills,
In the swinging and the clattering
  And the rattling of the cars?

               THOMAS DUNN ENGLISH.

YE MEANER BEAUTIES.

YE meaner beauties of the night,
  That poorly satisfy our eyes,
More by your numbers than your light:
  Ye common people of the skies!
  What are you when the moon shall rise?

Ye violets that first appear,
  By your pure purple mantles known,
Like the proud virgins of the year,
  As if the Spring were all your own!
  What are you when the rose is blown?

Ye curious chanters of the wood,
  That warble forth Dame Nature's lays,
Thinking your passions understood
  By your weak accents!—what's your praise
  When Philomel her voice shall raise?

So when my mistress shall be seen
  In sweetness of her looks and mind,
By virtue first, then choice, a queen:
  Tell me, if she was not designed
  Th' eclipse and glory of her kind?

SIR HENRY WOTTON.

THE REVERIE OF POOR SUSAN.

At the corner of Wood Street, when daylight appears,
Hangs a thrush that sings loud — it has sung for three years:
Poor Susan has passed by the spot, and has heard
In the silence of morning the song of the bird.

'T is a note of enchantment! what ails her? She sees
A mountain ascending, a vision of trees;
Bright volumes of vapor through Lothbury glide,
And a river flows on through the vale of Cheapside.

Green pastures she views, in the midst of the dale
Down which she so often has tripped with her pail;
And a single small cottage, a nest like a dove's,
The one only dwelling on earth that she loves.

She looks — and her heart is in heaven! But they fade:
The mist and the river, the hill and the shade.
The stream will not flow, and the hill will not rise,
And the colors have all passed away from her eyes.

WILLIAM WORDSWORTH.

INDEX OF FIRST LINES.

160 .   INDEX OF FIRST LINES.

www.ingramcontent.com/pod-product-compliance
Lightning Source LLC
Chambersburg PA
CBHW031116020726
47495CB00007B/2224